DOD-24

SO-BTB-036

Ohio Reading Circle
1979 6th

THE
FLEA MARKET
MYSTERY

THE FLEA MARKET MYSTERY

Virginia B. Evansen

Illustrated by Ray Abel

DODD, MEAD & COMPANY
NEW YORK

Copyright © 1978 by Virginia B. Evansen
All rights reserved
No part of this book may be reproduced in any form
without permission in writing from the publisher
Printed in the United States of America

1   2   3   4   5   6   7   8   9   10

Library of Congress Cataloging in Publication Data

Evansen, Virginia Besaw.
The flea market mystery.

SUMMARY: A robbery at a senior citizens' co-op sends
Nancy and Tomás Pérez from the Los Olivos flea market to a
boardwalk arcade in a search for the thieves of their
grandparents' handcrafted goods.
[1. Mystery and detective stories] I. Abel, Ray.
II. Title
PZ7.E893Fl   [Fic]   77–16863
ISBN 0–396–07521–5

JF
E9268f

To Virginia Ann, Patricia, and Nancy

1

The October air felt nippy as I hurried the six blocks from school to my grandparents' house. It had been a bad day, as had been all of the days since school started. My cheeks still burned from the embarrassment I had suffered during English class. I'd known the answer to Mrs. Bunton's question; I just couldn't get it out. The giggles from the girl sitting next to me hadn't helped, either.

I hurried through the door, heading for the comfort of the warm kitchen and the cookie jar. "Where are you, *Abuelita?*" I called. "I'm hungry."

"Out here." Grandmother was in the kitchen, sitting at the table. Tears were streaming down her cheeks.

I stopped just inside the door. I had never seen my grandmother cry before, and I felt as if the floor had tilted under my feet. I sort of tippy-toed over to her, put out my hand, and then let it fall to my side.

I looked at *mi abuelo*. My grandfather was pacing back and forth across the big, old-fashioned kitchen, setting down each foot with an angry stamp. His tall, thin frame was tense, his usually pleasant face furrowed with lines.

"What's the matter? What happened?" I asked.

"Some thieves broke into the Co-op Store and took almost everything there, Nancy. All of your grandmother's sweaters and afghans," he answered.

I moved closer to my grandmother and put my arm around her shoulder. I knew how happy my grandparents had been when the Senior Citizens' Cooperative Store had opened during the summer. They had both worked hard to make things to sell there on consignment.

"All of your grandfather's leather purses and belts were taken, too. I don't know what we are going to do. We needed the money for a new roof," Grandmother said. Her voice sounded hopeless.

"You can make more, *Abuelita*. You crochet so fast."

"No, Nancy. I can't spare the extra money for the yarn. When I sell an afghan, I buy yarn for the next one. The profit goes into the roof fund."

I looked longingly at the cookie jar. I was always hungry after school, but I didn't think that mentioning cookies would be a good idea when my grandparents were so upset. I wished I could do something to help—something besides giving Grandmother a hug. I wanted to buy a pile of yarn as big as a mountain for her.

"Maybe Tomás will know what to do," I said. "He'll be here soon. My brother always has good ideas."

"What can a fifteen-year-old boy do that the police can't?" Grandfather asked scornfully.

I hadn't thought about the police. "*They'll* find the robbers and get everything back. It will be all right." I patted Grandmother's shoulder.

"Mrs. Lancet, the manager, called the police first thing this morning when she opened the store and discovered the robbery. They told her that the stolen goods had probably been taken to Los Angeles to be sold. They held little hope of getting anything back. We aren't the only victims. Bill Jackson lost over three hundred dollars' worth of his handmade jewelry," Grandfather said.

Mr. Jackson was a long-time friend and neighbor. He had taken up jewelry-making as a hobby after he retired from the post office. I remembered hearing him say that his sales helped pay his taxes.

"Maybe your things are right here in Santo Rosario. The police should look around," I protested. "Anyway, I'm going to walk toward the high school to meet

Tomás. He might have an idea."

I ran out of the house and down the steps. I just couldn't stay in the kitchen a moment longer watching my grandmother cry. I had never seen her look defeated before. She was tiny and always busy, and so quick that she reminded me of a miniature whirlwind. Her hair, piled high on her head, was thick and still almost all black. She had large brown eyes that could snap when we misbehaved. She was a beautiful grandmother—*una abuela muy linda.*

When I reached the sidewalk, I turned and looked at the house. The white paint around the windows gleamed against the gray siding. The ornate gingerbread trim on the porch was clean, dusted by my grandmother each week. The eight-room house was really too large for my grandparents but I knew that they loved it and wouldn't be happy living anywhere else. The house had been built by my grandfather's grandfather almost a hundred years ago. One of the oldest houses in Santo Rosario, it was known as the Pérez House.

I sighed and started down the street which was lined with acacia trees, walking slowly past the old Victorian houses toward the high school. For almost as long as I could remember I had been going to my grandparents' house after school. My mother worked as a supervisor at an electronics plant and my father owned a florist shop. They picked us up around six each evening. On week nights they often didn't stop in but just waved to my grandparents, because Mom was anxious to get home and start dinner. Usually we spent part of our Sundays together.

At times I wished I could go to my own home after school as Jean Lewis, my best friend, did—to my own room where I could play records or just lie on my bed and look at the flowered wallpaper and let my thoughts drift. When school started, a month ago, I told my mother that now that I was thirteen I was old enough to come home after school and that I could help her by starting dinner.

"No, Nancy," Mom said in the firm voice that meant no arguing. "Thirteen's still young. When you are at Grandmother Pérez's house, I don't worry about you. Besides, you need to keep up your Spanish."

That sounded funny coming from my red-haired Irish mother who knew only a few words of Spanish. She always claimed she was going to take a night-school course in the language if she ever found the time. But she had insisted that we grow up bilingual, so we had learned Spanish from our grandparents. While both of them spoke English well, in their home they spoke nothing but Spanish unless they had guests. Tomás and I had learned the language in self-defense. We called our grandparents *Abuelo* and *Abuelita*, Grandfather and Little Grandmother.

The memory of *Abuelita's* tears quickened my steps as I turned the corner. Halfway down the block I saw Tomás walking slowly with Pete Higgins and Jim Block. I hurried up to them and told my brother I had to talk to him.

He waved me away. "Later," he said. "We're busy now."

"This is important," I insisted. "We have to talk before we reach *Abuelita's* house." I made it plain that I wanted to speak to my brother privately. I wasn't going to discuss family business in front of his friends, even though I had known Pete Higgins ever since I could remember. Jim Block was new in town and I didn't like him, although Tomás said he was an okay guy.

"Better listen to the kid's problem. That's what big brothers are for. She probably busted her doll buggy and wants you to fix it," Jim said, then doubled up with laughter over what he thought was a terrific joke.

I mentally pictured him as a horned toad with warts growing out of warts. "Come on, Tomás," I said. "This is serious."

We walked away from the two boys, and I told Tomás about the robbery. "*Abuelita's* whole world is broken," I finished. "They need that money to fix the roof. We have to do something *pronto*."

By this time we had reached the house. Tomás removed the headband he had taken to wearing during school hours. In the last couple of months he had become extremely ancestor conscious. He insisted that we call him Tomás instead of the Thomas he had been christened. He had taken to reading all kinds of books about early California history and studying Apache lore. That accounted for the headband.

"We must have some Indian ancestors," he had said. "I have a better right to wear a headband than lots of guys I know."

Grandfather Pérez had gone through the roof the first time Tomás came up with that theory. "My ancestors were soldiers who came to Santo Rosario with the Mission Fathers. There are records that Alvardo Pérez came to this city in 1791. And before that his father came from Spain to Mexico."

I could understand Grandfather's pride in his name, but I couldn't follow Tomás' reasoning. We were of Mexican and Irish descent. If he insisted on wearing a headband, it seemed logical to me that he should carry a shillelagh, too.

Anyway, Grandfather ruled in his own house so Tomás always took off the headband before he went inside. Now he leaned against the porch pillar and looked at me thoughtfully.

"So the police don't offer much hope," he said. "That's typical. Ever see a cop around when you need one?"

Since I had never needed a police officer, I couldn't see what the remark had to do with our problem and I told Tomás so. "We must figure out a way to help them."

"Maybe the parents can come up with the money for the roof."

"Yes, and if they did, you know that Grandfather would refuse it," I answered, impatient with a suggestion that I knew was impractical. My grandfather was a proud man.

Tomás looked at the house. I knew he had the same thoughts as I. We knew every nook and cranny from the attic stuffed with chests, trunks, and barrels to the basement, unusual in Santo Rosario dwellings, where Grandfather kept his leatherworking tools. We had spent so much of our time there that it was home to us.

"I'll just bet the loot is right here in Santo Rosario," Tomás said. "I can't imagine that a big gang of crooks with a truck would bother with a small operation like the Senior Citizens' Co-op here."

"You'd be surprised at how much some of the things sell for," I answered. "*Abuelita's* sweaters and afghans were priced at fifty to one hundred and twenty dollars. And there were Grandfather's leather belts and Mr. Jackson's jewelry. Remember that hammered silver bracelet I wanted? Forty-five dollars. There's no way I could save up for it with an allowance of only three dollars a week."

"That's it!" Tomás cried. "Our allowances. We can give your three and my five to Grandmother. Then she can buy yarn with the money."

I shook my head. "I don't think she'd take it. Besides, what would we do for lunch money?"

"It won't hurt us to go without. The Indians used to fast. They believed it benefitted the body and spirit."

"You and your ideas. Going without lunch would mean you'd clean out Grandmother's refrigerator after school."

Tomás opened the front door. "Speaking of food, what's the condition of the cookie jar?"

"It didn't seem appropriate to ask *Abuelita* for cookies when she was crying. Don't you go doing it," I warned.

"That's dumb. We need to get her mind off her troubles." With that Tomás roared into the house like an Apache brave. He pulled Grandmother off her chair, gave her a big kiss, and told her his stomach was screaming for food. "They had tacos in the cafeteria at lunch," he said. "Imagine serving a Pérez tacos so bad that my taste buds convulsed. You'll have to go over there and give the cooks a lesson in taco-making."

Grandmother brightened. She poured two glasses of milk and set out a plate of cookies while Tomás questioned Grandfather about the robbery.

"It seems that the cops are taking the easy way out," Tomás argued, reaching for a cookie. "If they decide the thieves are hundreds of miles away, they won't have to spend time looking for them here."

"The police know what they are doing," Grandfather said. "Besides, no one would dare to sell the items in Santo Rosario."

"This is a tourist town with dozens of shops handling artsy-craftsy goods. If you spread the things out among the stores, no one would recognize them as stolen," Tomás insisted.

"I would. I'd know my afghans anywhere. Your grandfather's belts, too." Grandmother's dark eyes flashed as she looked at Tomás.

I knew she was right. She made her own patterns, adapting them from Mexican and Indian designs. She finished the edges with a special stitch and signed each piece with a tiny monogram in the corner. That was why her sweaters and afghans brought so much money.

Tomás polished off the cookies while we waited for our parents. As soon as we were in the car, I told Mom and Dad about the burglary. "We have to do something," I finished. "Grandmother needs that money for a new roof."

"Stealing from anyone is a crime, but stealing from old people who live on pensions is hideous," Dad said in a furious voice. "I'd like to get my hands on them. I'd teach them not to take other people's property if I had to break every one of their fingers into ten pieces."

"That won't help your parents," Mom said. She was silent for a couple of blocks. I looked out at the darkening sky and fear gathered behind my chest. My parents *had* to come up with a solution. They had always had the answers before.

"We could take the money out of the college fund, Juan," Mom said to my father. "We have a few years before Tomás starts college, and I'll save some extra dollars each week to make it up."

"You know as well as I do, *machree*, that my father's stubborn Spanish pride wouldn't permit him to take a penny from us." The affectionate Irish word always sounded strange coming from my father's lips. Somehow I always expected him to say *querida* or *mi novia*, but he called her *machree* or some other Irish endearment.

"You could insist," my mother said gently. "Families should help in times of trouble."

"No, I couldn't. Father's a proud man. *Mucho hombre.*"

"Please, Juan. We must help them. You could offer to lend them the money," Mom insisted.

"All right. We'll be pinched because our property taxes went up twenty per cent and are due in December, but I'll try to make Father accept the money as a loan."

As soon as the car stopped, I dashed into the kitchen and started setting the table for dinner. My head felt like a food blender with thoughts splashing against my skull. What were we going to do? I knew that my grandfather would refuse the money. I had heard him say too many times that he owed no man and was proud of it. If Mom and Dad couldn't help, Tomás and I would have to find the stolen goods or a way to make money. But how?

2

After wiping the dinner dishes, I took my books to my room, sat down at my desk, and stared at my government assignment. We were studying the Constitution. What a dreadful thing, I thought bitterly, unable to concentrate. Stealing from older people. Robbing a store operated by senior citizens who desperately needed extra income.

I remembered Mrs. Johnson. She did spool weaving with fingers so swollen from arthritis that my stomach twisted when I saw them. But she always had a smile on her face. She told me that she'd taken up spool weaving to exercise her fingers, that sometimes it hurt to use them and she didn't want them to stiffen. She lived on a small pension and she needed the money from selling her work.

I was so furious at the burglars that I hit my book

with my hand. I rubbed my smarting palm against my cheek and slumped in my chair. What you'd like to do, Nancy Pérez, I whispered to myself, is run up to Grandmother and Grandfather and hand them five hundred silver dollars. Yes, and there's pie in the sky, too.

I stood up, slid out of my jeans and sweater, opened the closet, and reached for my robe. I wrestled with the hanger, trying to get the robe out of the bulging closet. Dresses, skirts, pants, tops, and coats were jammed in so tightly that the hangers were squeezed together, with some of them tangled. Slippers and shoes, most of them too small, covered the floor. Boxes of games sat on the shelf at the top of the closet, reaching almost to the ceiling. I turned and looked at the toy chest sitting at the foot of my bed. It had been a birthday present when I was six, and I used it now as extra seating space and a place for my bedspread at night. I knew, without raising the lid, that outgrown dolls and old toys filled it to the top.

The glimmer of an idea danced in my head. "You must get rid of some of that junk," my mother had said last week. "There are many boys and girls who need clothes. Sort some out and I'll take them to the Goodwill. They've been asking for donations."

I had shaken my head stubbornly. "They are mine, and I want to keep them."

"But what can you do with shoes that are three sizes too small?" she asked.

"They'll come in handy for something."

"You're just like your grandmother," my mother said. "A pack rat and a hopeless pack rat at that. I'll bet she doesn't even know what she has stored in that attic of hers."

I had kept quiet. I saw no point in antagonizing my mother any further. I didn't want her to issue an ultimatum.

"You know you can't wear half the clothes in that closet. They are too small. If you want anything new for Christmas, you're going to have to clear out those old things."

"I'll pack some of them away," I promised.

Mom had looked defeated. "I don't understand these squirrelly tendencies," she'd said.

I couldn't explain. Something inside me wouldn't let me part with my belongings. To do so felt almost as if I were giving away a part of myself. I pulled out a blue dress I'd worn in the fifth grade. I had grown so fast that year that I'd only worn it a few times— once when the school chorus gave an afternoon performance. Mom and Mrs. Lewis had been in the audience, smiling at Jean and me the whole time.

Afterward Mom told me that the chorus was great but that she thought the orchestra was a bit off-key.

On the way out I heard the mother of the violinist saying that the orchestra was great but that she thought the chorus had been flat on two songs. I guess a great performance depends on parental viewpoint.

Mom had been made a supervisor the next fall. After that she stopped coming to daytime school performances. "I have a responsibility to my employer," she explained. "I have to set a good example for the people working for me, and I can't take time off unless it's important."

I guess my being in the sixth-grade play didn't fit her idea of really important. It wasn't a big deal. I was one of the witches in the first scene. I didn't have any lines, but I would have liked Mom to watch me stir the caldron. Jean told me later that I'd held my elbows high in the manner of an *artiste*.

That's what Jean was planning to be. An *artiste*. A *tragedienne* in the grand manner of Sarah Bernhardt. I thought privately that Jean was a little dumpy for such ambition, but maybe the years would improve her figure.

I looked at the closet again. Maybe Mom was right. Cleaning it out might be a step toward the maturity that my teachers claimed I lacked. And it might be a step to something else. The stuff was all good. Hardly worn at all. There were all of those boxes of games that we never used. Some of them almost new.

The glimmer became full blown. I buttoned my robe and raced down the hall to Tomás' room. He was bent over his desk working on the old radio he was trying to repair. I waited until he looked up at me, then asked if he'd had any ideas about our grandparents' problems.

Tomás shook his head. "No."

"I have a great idea. Why don't we have a garage sale?"

My brother's dark eyes met mine. "People do make money at garage sales, but would we have enough stock to make one worthwhile?"

"There's my closet and all those toys, games, and books that we haven't touched for years."

"Has Mom sent off the odds and ends she made me clear out of my closet yet?"

"I think they're still in the garage. Along with our old bikes."

Tomás put down his screwdriver. "We'll do it! We'll make a mint of money and give it all to Grandfather."

"Do you think he'll take the money?" I asked doubtfully. "Remember how sure Dad was that he wouldn't accept a loan."

"This is different. We'll just be getting rid of old stuff we can't use."

"That's right," I agreed. "Grandfather will take the money because making it from a garage sale is like finding money." I sounded more confident than I felt.

"Sure he will. But we'll have to do a lot of planning."

"Do you really think we can swing a garage sale by ourselves?" I asked.

"Of course." Tomás was almost whispering. "We'll scout a bunch of garage sales to see how they do things and check prices. There's something else we can do at the same time, and *that's* keep an eye out for belts and afghans."

I stared at my brother. "You don't really think we'll find them here in Santo Rosario?"

"It's possible, but it's more likely that those *bandidos* will try to get rid of the loot at the Los Olivos flea market. We ought to go there, too."

"How could we get there?" We'd been to the Los Olivos flea market once, three years ago. It was huge. Acres and acres of junk for sale. Everything from antiques to tools to zithers. But it was thirty miles from Santo Rosario over a twisty mountain range.

"Maybe we could get the parents to take us."

I hated to ice the idea. "Mom's usually tired and wants to rest on Sundays."

"I know." Tomás was silent for a moment. "That's the worst part about being only fifteen and a sophomore. All of my friends are sixteen and already driving."

24

"It's not your fault you were accelerated," I said, pronouncing the word carefully.

"It's all right most of the time." Tomás sounded bitter. "But when the rest of the guys start driving it's not much fun using a ten-speed."

"It's good for the ecology and saves gas," I said, trying to make a joke.

"Maybe I could talk Jim Block into taking us," Tomás said.

I made a face. "Too bad Pete's folks won't let him use their car yet."

"They're being sticky about his earning the money for the extra insurance premium. I'll try Jim. He's a pretty good guy and always has access to a car when he wants it."

"You don't know him very well, do you, Tomás?"

"Well, you know his family moved here just before school started." Tomás' eyes met mine thoughtfully. "We do a lot of yakking about the parents' rules, but you know something, I think we are luckier than Jim is. His parents never seem to care what he does, where he goes, or when he comes home. He's really a lonely guy."

I flared up. I knew Tomás was intensely loyal to his friends but that remark about the doll buggy had rankled. "He's always trying to make smart jokes. Especially at my expense."

"That's his way of trying to get in with the crowd. Maybe even a way of impressing you. Come on. Let's ask the parents about the garage sale."

Mom and Dad were in the living room, sitting close together on the couch. Mom looked at me incredulously while Tomás explained what we had in mind. "I'm for anything that will get you to clean out that closet," she said when he finished.

"I just don't know," Dad said slowly. "You know your mother does my bookkeeping on Saturdays. Can you two handle a project like this by yourselves?"

"Why not?" Tomás asked. "We're perfectly capable of making change and selling things and talking to people."

"I hear that garage sales attract mobs of people," Mom said. "Without adult supervision, you could get into trouble. What would you do if someone asked to use the bathroom or the telephone?"

"Why, let them," I answered.

Mom gestured helplessly at Dad. "You see?"

I stared from one to the other. "What's wrong with that?"

"You would be letting someone into the house."

"But, Mom, people come to garage sales to buy things, not steal," I protested.

"You can't be certain they won't pocket something if they have a chance," she said.

26

"You could give us some rules, and we'd go by them," Tomás suggested. "We could ask our friends to help."

"That sounds better. Your idea is excellent, and if it means that Nancy cleans out her closet, I'm sure your mother is in favor of it. Besides, your grandfather might come over to supervise. Why not ask him?" Dad said.

"It's all right with me if Grandfather Pérez will help," Mom agreed. "Your plans sound good, especially the part about investigating garage sales to see how things are priced. When would you want to hold yours?"

I looked at my brother. "Maybe about a week from Saturday?"

Tomás nodded. "That gives us all day Saturday to see what happens at these sales, and on Sunday we want to go to the Los Olivos flea market if Jim Block can take us."

"Jim Block—that new boy you brought home last week?" Mom asked. "Is he a good driver?"

"Oh, yes," Tomás answered. "I've ridden with him a couple of times. He's careful."

Dad laid a hand on Mom's arm. "It sounds okay to me," he said. "As long as you are home by dark."

Tomás' face was grim as we walked back to his room. " 'Is he a good driver?' " he repeated. "Next thing you know she'll be wanting to meet his parents before she lets us ride with him."

"You're not being fair. Remember what you said about Jim's parents," I said, trying to calm him down. Tomás had been prickly ever since school started. I wondered if being in high school was as much fun as I thought it would be.

"At least we've made a start," Tomás said. "Be sure to get all your homework finished before Saturday so we have the whole week end free."

I nodded and went into my room, ignored the government book, and tackled a theme for English. What I wanted to write about was the heartbreak caused by the burglary. What I had for a topic, assigned by Mrs. Bunton, was "How Thoreau Would Feel Today." Could I combine Thoreau and the burglars and say that he would be against them? I sighed. It would probably be all right with Thoreau, but not with Mrs. Bunton.

An hour later I crawled into bed and pulled the quilt up around my shoulders. *Mi abuelita* would smile when she heard what we planned, I thought happily. Then happiness fizzled as I thought of Sunday. While I wanted to go to the Los Olivos flea market, I wasn't sure I wanted to go with Jim Block. Mom's question came into my mind. We really didn't know much about him. Even if he didn't mean anything by them, his jokes were cruel. I shivered. Tomás' friends had always been nice to me. Maybe because they knew Tomás wouldn't stand for anything else. But Jim was different, and I really didn't like him.

3

The week dragged. School isn't all that it's cracked up to be when you're in the eighth grade. The teachers are so busy getting you ready for high school that they make you take the subjects in big gulps. That's okay for people like Tomás and Jean whose brains absorb books at a glance. I'm the dull, plodding type who reads each paragraph three times and then isn't quite certain what it says and whose tongue twists even when the answer is on the tip.

Jean read for the lead in the class play and was highly insulted when she was given the comic role. Since she's the Marlo Thomas type, I thought the casting appropriate, but Jean was indignant.

"That Mary Ellen Seeley looks slinky, but she can't project," she declared.

"You don't project so well yourself," I said bluntly. "Give yourself a few years and more experience."

"At least I have a part," Jean said in an offended voice.

I realized I had hurt her feelings. "It's a good part, too," I consoled. "If you work at it, you'll probably steal the play from Mary Ellen."

Jean brightened. "Say, have you found out anything more about that robbery at your grandparents' Co-op?"

"No. Are you coming with us Saturday when we go to the garage sales?"

"I sure am. In fact, my mother said I could help with yours. She said it would be a real experience for me."

"That's usually what mothers say when they mean you're in for a bunch of hard work." I pushed my hair back. "Well, Saturday may get here yet."

Saturday morning finally did arrive. Tomás and I were out of bed by seven. Jean wheeled up on her ten-speed at quarter of eight and Pete Higgins was right behind her. Tomás had made a list of all twenty-two garage and yard sales being held that morning and handed each one of us a pencil and small notebook. It seemed that Tomás always planned ahead. I would have gone off empty handed.

"Jean, you record prices of clothes and jewelry. Nancy, you do dishes, and Pete and I will look at books, toys, and tools." Tomás gave the orders as if he were an Indian chief sending out a war party.

I nodded. I'd price dishes all right, but I made up my

mind that I was going to keep my eyes open for crocheted sweaters and afghans.

"You and Pete should look for handmade leather items, too," I suggested to Tomás. "You would certainly recognize anything Grandfather had made."

"I sure would, but I don't think we'll find the stuff at a garage sale."

I shoved the notebook into the purse slung over my shoulder and reached for my bike. "Why not? The police can't check every garage sale in this town for stolen merchandise."

The four of us raced down the street to the first

address on Tomás' list where a five-family sale was scheduled. From the number of cars in front of the house, it looked as if they had advertised free popcorn and door prizes. I pushed through the crowd to a table filled with lamps, vases, and glassware.

A lot of it was chipped and cracked. The prices ranged from twenty-five cents to a dollar. I reached for a dull green vase, but a woman in a red jacket snatched it up just as I touched it.

"I knew it," she whispered excitedly to her taller companion as she turned it over. "I knew it by that soft glaze. Here's the mark. It's Rookwood and only a

dollar. Jenny Long at the Early Times Shoppe will give me ten for it in a minute."

"*Cochina,*" I muttered, thinking she even looked like a pig, and moved over to a table heaped with sweaters. Shrunken and worn out. At least my outgrown things were in good shape and should be worth more than the quarter price tag on these.

Tomás flapped his hand at me, and we all hopped on our bikes. When we reached the next address the whispering woman in the red jacket was already there, haggling with the seller about the price of a plate. I made a note that some people tried to bargain. We had better decide what to do about that before our sale.

Shortly after noon we were finished with the garage sales. I had seen lots of chipped and cracked junk, but loads of good things, too. Some of the sales had been moving sales. At one place an old man, aided by a woman who was obviously his daughter, was selling all of his possessions. The whispering woman, who had come here too, had gathered up a box of vases, pictures, knick-knacks, and dishes. As the wrinkled old man took the three dollars from her, his face filled with distress. He turned to his daughter. "Couldn't you keep some of these things? After all, they were your mother's."

She flicked a bit of dust from her white pants suit and lifted her eyebrows. "Father, please," she said.

"We've been through all that. You know they don't fit my décor and your room isn't large enough for another thing. Not with all those books you've already moved to my house."

Pobrecito, I thought. He probably won't fit her décor, either.

Tomás came up to me and suggested that we go home, pack some sandwiches, and go to the beach. "We can discuss what we've learned and lay out plans for tomorrow," he said.

The beach was my favorite place. Not the sand in front of the boardwalk which was always littered with tourists, but a quiet spot a mile to the south where rocks jutting through the sand provided backrests. The beach was where I went when I was happy and when I was sad. Somehow problems didn't loom so large when one thought about them at the edge of the Pacific Ocean.

4

The Los Olivos flea market was just as I remembered it. Acres of cars parked in the blazing sun. What seemed like miles of stalls, makeshift booths, card tables, picnic tables, and tarps spread on the ground, all covered with merchandise. People in our area had a saying, "If you can't find it at the Los Olivos flea market, it hasn't been made," and I believed it. The place was like a hundred garage sales with a county fair tossed in for good measure. Kids ran by with cones of cotton candy blooming like roses in their fists, a giant Great Dane pulled his mistress along on a red leather leash, pushcart vendors bawled the merits of hot dogs and ice-cold beer.

"I could use one right now," Jim Block said, eyeing the beer cart.

"You know we can't buy that stuff," Tomás answered.

"It's easy to get. What'll you bet I can have my hands on a long, tall beer in five minutes?" Jim's smile was a dare.

"Yeah, and five seconds later you'll have one of the security guys all over you."

I hoped Jim was just putting us on, but I wasn't too sure. "Let's get started," I said. "The way you laid it out, Tomás, the third and fourth rows are mine and the fifth and sixth rows are Jean's."

"Right. I'll take the first two and Jim the seventh and eighth. I wish Pete could have come. That would have meant two more rows covered the first time through, but he had two lawn-mowing jobs. Remember, up one side and back the other with each row. Then we'll meet right here."

I nodded, and Jean and I started down our rows. I walked past stall after stall filled with tools, pipes, electrical supplies, and bathroom fixtures without paying too much attention. These stalls were all roofed over, as were the next five which were filled with what the signs said were antiques. I was in the section of permanent flea market dealers where the stalls were like miniature shops complete with signs—"The Old Shoe," "The Cupboard"—over the gates.

Inside the "Blue Pelican" I paused at a table near the back filled with glittering glassware and gasped at the price tag on a tumbler. Seven dollars. I was certain I had seen one like it before. I turned to the owner of the stall who was hovering nervously nearby.

"Why is this one worth so much?" I asked, reaching for it.

"Don't touch that, kid!" she snapped. "It's an antique."

As I pulled my hand back, I stumbled and grabbed for the edge of the table.

She jerked me away and pushed me toward the front of the stall. "Get along," she said through her teeth. "You kids are always breaking things or stealing. Get away."

"But I just—" I broke off as she gave me a shove.

"Want me to call security?" she threatened.

A couple of people were looking at me. I could feel my face getting hot, and I turned toward the next stall.

"All the child did was ask a question," protested a young woman who had been standing on the other side of the table.

"Child, nothing. A teen-ager. Teen-agers are nothing but trouble. Smash things, rob a person blind, take up my attention with stupid questions while behind my back someone lifts a piece of stock. Why, last week I lost—"

The woman's voice followed me. It seemed as if her throat were equipped with amplifiers. The next stall was filled with table after table covered with books. I like books, but I didn't stop to look. The man behind the counter had heard every word the acid-tongued antique woman had shouted, and he was looking at me as if he expected me to rip off half his stock.

My face was burning and I was so mad I was almost ready to cry. It was always that way. Go into a store and eyes followed you everywhere. And the wait. Adults were always waited upon first. So I didn't have seven dollars! I did have three dollars in the pocket of my jeans. That glass. I knew I had seen one like it, but where? Then the memory of the whispering woman at the garage sales yesterday returned. There had been a gloating look on her face when she bought three glasses like that one from the poor old man who was going to go live with his daughter. She'd only paid ten cents each for them.

I walked on slowly down the row, jotting down prices, thinking hard as I passed tables of pillows, handmade quilts, more books, rusty iron frying pans, and a litter of German shepherd puppies with a sign saying "Free to a Good Home."

When I reached the end of the row, I crossed to the other side, wishing that Jean and I had paired up instead of each taking a row. My steps lagged as I neared the antique stalls. If that crow of a woman who owned the "Blue Pelican" saw me, she would probably start screeching again. I sidled by, keeping my back to the witch's shop, and reached the end where I found Jim leaning against a power pole. He was drinking from a tall paper cup swathed in a napkin. I saw foam around his mouth as he lifted his head.

"Just taking a lemonade break, little sister," he said when he saw me staring at him. "It's too hot for all this cops and robbers stuff." He crumpled the cup and stuffed it into a trash can.

I gave him my Dracula glare as he ambled down the middle of his second row, glancing rapidly from side to side. Why, he couldn't possibly spot anything from the Co-op walking that fast, and he wouldn't see any prices, either. I decided to wait for Jean. We could work together, each taking a side of a row.

Jean's feet dragged as she came around the corner of a stall, and I saw that her face was red. "I wish I'd remembered a hat," she said. "It's hot for October, and I'm getting sunburned. I wish I were a brunette, like you."

I stared at her in surprise. "Why? I've always wanted fair skin like yours."

"You don't know what a hassle skin like mine is," she said bitterly. "Always chapped, sunburned, or freckled. And my hair always frizzes. Yours is so nice and heavy and straight."

I felt embarrassed. For years I had envied Jean her light skin and the blonde hair that curled gently around her face. I had to admit that she looked hot. Her face was just plain red, and there was a big freckle on the tip of her nose. "Let's each take a side of my row, here," I suggested. "Then we'll share yours. That way we can at least wave at each other."

Jean agreed and we started. I made a couple of notes about the prices of used games. Higher than I would have thought. I realized we would have to be careful about our pricing. As I neared the end of the row I saw Jim leaning against the back of a blue-and-white station wagon talking to a scrawny young man. Jim had another paper cup in his hand. I started forward furiously, ready to shout at him. If he thought I was going to ride in a car with a driver full of beer, he could think again. Then I noticed the table in front of the wagon. A girl with heavy, reddish-orange braids tied at the ends with purple yarn stood behind it. Crocheted sweaters, scarves, and afghans covered the table.

I stopped, dodged back, and bent over a display of books. Jim hadn't seen me. I wondered what he was doing and glanced sideways with my head bent as he walked around the corner, tossing the cup on the ground in front of the display table.

I couldn't see Jean and I wished frantically that I knew where Tomás was. Then I saw the scrawny-faced man say something to the girl. She turned and started throwing armloads of the crocheted things into the wagon. I spotted Jean across the aisle, yelled at her, and then ran for the table.

"We're closed," the girl snapped, tossing the last pieces of merchandise into the car. The gray-and-orange afghan on top was edged with a familiar stitch. I was sure that my grandmother had made it. I pushed closer as the man folded the table and shoved it into the back of the wagon. "Hey!" I yelled. "I want to buy that one."

The girl ran to the front of the car without saying a word. They pulled out, racing the engine and honking to scatter the people in the way.

Jean dashed up to me. "What's the matter?"

"They had one of Grandmother's afghans. I'm sure they did," I said.

"Did you get the license number?"

I hadn't thought of that. I started to run after the car, then stopped, realizing that I couldn't catch it. *Estúpida* I muttered, furious with myself. Just as dumb as always. I pulled my notebook out of my shoulder bag and wrote down "blue-and-white station wagon." But was it old or new? And what make? I didn't know a Ford from a Buick about cars.

I turned to Jean. "The man was scrawny faced and the girl had long reddish-orange braids tied with yarn."

"A lot of good that does."

"Let's find Tomás. He'll know what to do." I started off and stepped on the paper cup Jim had dropped. I picked it up and peeled off the napkin. Just as I had suspected. Beer. I grabbed Jean's arm. The faster we found Tomás, the better.

5

Tomás had almost reached the end of his row when we caught up to him. I dodged around a couple of bargain hunters and grabbed his arm. Just as I started to tell him about the station-wagon people and the afghan, I saw Jim coming from the other direction. He held a belt in his hand.

"I bought this from an old couple three rows over," he said. "I don't know much about leatherwork but it looked good, and I needed a belt. Do you think it could be one your grandfather made?"

I stared suspiciously at Jim while Tomás took the belt from him. Had he had something in his hand when he walked away from that station wagon? I remembered seeing him toss the cup on the ground, but I couldn't be certain he had been carrying anything. It was strange that those people had decided to leave right after Jim talked to them. Was it possible that he had warned them? That Jim was involved in the robbery?

Tomás looked at the buckle. "My grandfather uses this kind," he said. Then he inspected the smooth leather under the buckle carefully. "Yes, it is his! See this small *p?* It stands for Pérez. Grandfather and Grandmother are proud of their work. They always sign it." He handed the belt to Jim. "Come on. Show us where you bought this."

"Three rows over," Jim said. "I'd finished my rows so I thought I'd do a couple of extra ones."

"Can you find the place again?" I asked, wondering how Jim had had time to finish his rows.

"Easier than eating custard pie," he answered. "This way." He looked like a general in an old television movie leading the troops to battle as he strutted in front of us. I grabbed Jean's arm and we hurried to keep up with him. If Jim had bought the belt three rows down, then the couple in the station wagon couldn't have been involved in the robbery and neither could Jim. But why had they left so suddenly, and with so much unsold merchandise?

I decided to keep quiet until I could talk to Tomás privately. Jean pulled at my arm. "Aren't you going to tell them about the station wagon?" she asked.

"Not right now," I answered in a low voice.

"There's no hope of catching it, anyway."

"You could give the police a description of the car and the people. There can't be too many blue-and-white station wagons around loaded with crocheted items. The cops might be able to stop them, especially if they are headed back on the highway to Santo Rosario."

We were too close to Jim and Tomás for me to tell Jean of my suspicions. "Let's keep quiet and see what happens now," I whispered. Jim couldn't have been involved, I told myself. Surely he would have warned the station-wagon people to stay away, that we were coming to the flea market today, if he had had any connection with them.

Jim stopped and pointed at a booth run by an elderly couple. A white-haired lady sat behind a table filled with assorted glassware. The man, his face a map of wrinkles, leaned against a car that looked as old as he was. Suspended from a rope supported by two poles were five belts. While we watched, a lady stopped and bought one.

"That's the place," Jim said. "Looks like the evidence is disappearing fast. Well, you don't need me here. I'm hungry. I'll get something to eat and meet you back at the car." With that he walked away before I could say a word.

"Go get someone from security," Tomás said to me

in an easy, level voice. "Quick, before they sell all the belts."

"Wait," Jean said. "Let's ask some questions first. You could be mistaken about the belt being your grandfather's."

"I know my grandfather's work," Tomás insisted.

"Still, it won't hurt to ask some questions. These people don't look like thieves," Jean argued.

We edged up to the table. I couldn't see anything knitted or crocheted so I sidled over to the old car and looked into the back. Nothing there. The trunk was open and filled with empty boxes. Tomás had moved to the belts and was examining a brown one.

"Give you a good price on that. Only three dollars," the old man said.

I gasped. Grandfather's belts were priced at seven-fifty to ten dollars in the Co-op.

"That's a mighty good price for a stolen belt!" Tomás' voice was hard. "Get security, Nancy."

"We don't deal in stolen merchandise," the man answered. "We bought them here this morning at a bargain. That's why I can sell them for three dollars each."

"They are stolen!" Tomás yelled. "Stolen from the Senior Citizens' Co-op in Santo Rosario where we live, and I can prove it." He turned to me. "Nancy, how does Grandfather sign his work?"

"With a small *p* for Pérez under the buckle," I said slowly, looking at the white-haired lady who had risen and come to stand beside her husband. Somehow she seemed familiar, like someone I had seen in a grocery store or at a restaurant, but I couldn't remember where.

"Look for yourself." Tomás held out the belt to the man. "It's marked the same way the one my friend just bought was marked."

The old man's face whitened as he stared down at the small *p*. "I should have known something was wrong," he said bitterly. "They were too cheap. Come on and I'll show you the people I bought them from. They have a blue-and-white station wagon. A man who claimed to have made the belts and a girl with braids . . ."

"They've gone," I interrupted.

"How do you know?" Tomás asked.

"That's what I started to tell you before Jim came up with the belt. The girl with the reddish-orange braids was throwing crocheted things into the station wagon. She said they were closed, and they tore out of here as if they were running from the police." I turned to the man. "The girl's hair, was it a light red?"

"Yes, it glowed in the sun, the same color as a new copper penny," the man answered.

"I'm Mrs. Olssen," the woman said. "Iris Olssen."

There were tears in her eyes and she reminded me of Grandmother. "We don't—"

Her husband put his hand on hers. "I'll take care of this, dear," he said. He looked straight at Tomás. "I'm Olaf Olssen. We live in Santo Rosario. We come here once every two months to sell things because our Social Security checks don't stretch far enough. But we don't deal in stolen goods. And we think people who would steal from a Senior Citizens' Co-op should have their faces pushed into the dirt and held there."

"We think so, too," Tomás said. "My grandfather does leatherwork to make money to pay for a new roof."

"There are four belts left," Mr. Olssen said. "I paid fifty cents each for eight. That was four dollars. I've sold half of them for twelve dollars altogether. If I give you eight dollars for your grandfather and the remaining belts, would it be all right?"

"I think that would be fair," Tomás said with a smile.

"I don't," Mrs. Olssen objected. "I think you should give him the whole twelve dollars."

Tomás shook his head. "Then you would be out four dollars of your own money. That wouldn't be fair, either."

"We don't deal in stolen goods," Mrs. Olssen said proudly, her eyes bright with the unshed tears. "I saw the way your friend looked at us before he left. He probably thinks we are thieves."

I had gone back to their table and was looking at a glass marked ten dollars. An idea popped into my head. "Maybe you could help us," I suggested. "Then it would be really fair."

"Help you. How?" Mrs. Olssen asked.

"We're planning a garage sale to help raise the money for Grandfather's roof, and we really don't know how to price things. That's part of the reason we came to the flea market," I explained.

"We'd be glad to help you," Mr. Olssen said with great dignity.

"What makes this glass worth so much?" I asked.

"It's pressed glass, Button Arches pattern," Mrs. Olssen answered.

"It's what?"

"It's an antique. Don't you know anything about antiques?" Mrs. Olssen asked.

I shook my head.

"If you'll come to my house after school tomorrow, I'll lend you some books," she offered. "We can make plans about your garage sale then, too." She told us her address, Mr. Olssen gave Tomás the belts and money, and we said good-bye.

"We'd better get some hot dogs on the way back to the car," Tomás suggested, handing me the belts.

"We'd better get back to the car before that stupid friend of yours has time to drink a gallon of beer," I snapped, as I rolled up the belts and stuffed them into my shoulder bag.

"Jim doesn't drink," Tomás said.

"I saw him drinking," I insisted. "If you think I'm going to ride with a driver full of beer, you've got beans in your skull. I'll call Mom and ask her to come and get us."

"But Jim doesn't drink. He's an absolutely straight guy."

"I saw him!" I was getting mad, really mad, and when I get mad, I cry, which makes me even madder.

"It must have been lemonade. I don't want to hear another word against him. He's *mi amigo.*"

"Well, you just smell your *amigo's* breath when we reach him. I'll bet it will be beery."

"Stop arguing, you two." Jean sounded impatient. "I'm starving, and I'm getting sunburned. Come on."

6

Jim was lounging against the front fender with a self-satisfied smirk on his face when we reached the car, mustard-smeared hot dogs in our fists. "Get in," he ordered. "It's only noon and there's still time for Tomás and me to get in some surfing."

Tomás threw me a triumphant look, and I didn't dare say a word. I just hoped I had been wrong, but as soon as we reached the freeway, I wished I had stayed out of that car and called my mother.

Even Tomás looked worried as Jim threw the car into the fast lane and stepped on the gas. "We aren't in that much of a hurry," he said. "No point in picking up a ticket."

Jim eased off a bit, but as soon as we started the eight-mile, winding climb to the summit he was back at it, changing lanes as he wove in and out of the slow traffic. "These guys drive like little old ladies on their way to a tea party," he snarled.

Jean squealed as we swung around a pickup truck and skidded close to the divider. "Slow down, Jim," Tomás yelled. "I told you we weren't in that much of a hurry."

Jim's answer was to push the car a little faster. "If you don't like my driving, you can get out and walk," he said.

I grabbed Jean's hand, and I prayed. Why, oh, why, had I been so stupid? Why hadn't I called Mom? So I didn't want Tomás angry with me. Why had I let him stop me when I *knew* that Jim had been drinking? How much beer had he guzzled, I wondered, as the car slewed around another curve.

The road from Los Olivos to Santo Rosario was dangerous and just now it was filled with cars headed for the beach. The people poured over the mountains every Saturday and Sunday loaded with beach towels, tanning lotion, and picnic baskets. And every Monday night we read in the paper about one or two pleasure seekers who had been killed because of fast driving on this highway.

Jim cut in short and we missed another car by inches. Jean screamed and then started to sob. "Pull over at the next turnout, Jim, and let me drive," Tomás ordered.

"You don't have a license, little boy." Jim's answer was a sneer. Jean's head was in my lap, and I had my arms around her. The rear end swerved as Jim went out around another car, and I saw the divider coming at us.

Metal screeched as the fender struck. We bounced back into the right-hand lane, just ahead of the car we were passing, then went sideways toward the bank. I heard tires squealing. Then everything went kind of hazy as the car spun around, bouncing off the bank to our right and back into traffic. A car hit us and whirled us around again, throwing Jean to the floor. Jean's screams dropped to a shrill keening that cut my ears. I heard mumbling about crazy, stupid, slow drivers from Jim, and I felt a sudden, sharp pain in my arm.

"Are you all right?" The voice belonged to a man looking down through the window. I realized that our car was on its side, that I was lying on top of Jean.

I muttered something. The man wrenched the door open and reached for my hand. I grabbed, and he pulled me up. Pain rocked through me, and I looked at my left arm, knowing it was broken.

I was dizzy, and I started to sit down, but the man led me to the edge of the highway. "Tomás," I said with a moan. "Help Tomás."

"We're getting them out," the man answered. I sank down to the ground, cradling my left arm with my right hand, trying to see through the group of people crowded around the car. Behind me I heard someone swearing, and I looked back at the wrecked front end of the car that had hit us. The driver sat on the edge of the pavement, holding a little girl in his lap. Blood streamed from her forehead, and the man cursed and cursed.

I turned back toward our car and saw men lifting Tomás out through the door. His eyes were closed and he was limp. I tried to get up, but a lady put her hand on my shoulder. "Stay still," she ordered.

"That's my brother." I tried to scream the words, but they came out in a low mumble.

"I'll go see how he is."

She returned in a moment holding my shoulder bag. "He's breathing all right, and the other boy doesn't appear to be hurt. Is this purse yours?"

I nodded. "That's Jim," I said. "Where is Jean?" In the distance I heard sirens. Maybe it was because I knew help was at hand, or maybe it was the pain catching up with me, but I felt myself sliding, sliding right off into darkness.

I awakened with a bright light shining in my eyes, and I started to cry. "I want my mother," I said through sobs. Oh, I did want my mother. And I wanted my father and I wanted to be home safe with them. Suddenly I was angry with Tomás. Where did he get that "he was always right" bit? He should have listened to me. Then I realized, bitterly, that I should have listened to myself. I should never have gotten into Jim's car. Nor should I have let Jean. No matter what Tomás said. Not even if we couldn't have had the garage sale. Not even if we lost the chance to help earn the roof money.

Maybe Jim would have had the accident anyway. Maybe even a worse one, but Jean and I wouldn't have been there. I wouldn't have this arm that felt as if a sword were buried in it, and Jean wouldn't be hurt or maybe dead.

I was crying harder when I felt a prick in my right arm. "Now, stop that," a voice said sharply. "I've given you something for pain, and you'll feel better soon. You aren't badly hurt. Just a fractured arm."

I looked up at a young nurse's face. "I know," I said. "But it was my fault."

"Don't talk," she ordered. "Go to sleep."

The knife-edged pain dulled, and I closed my eyes. I thought I heard Tomás' voice, but I couldn't be certain.

7

Being in an automobile accident does things to a
person. I found it hard to get into a car again,
even though my father was the driver and I was on my
way home from the Los Olivos General Hospital
where I had spent the night.

I had awakened the second time in a hospital bed,
nauseated, and with a plaster cast on my left arm. My
mother was standing beside me, her face showing her
love and concern.

"Tomás?" I asked.

"He's all right. Just a concussion. Your father is
with him," Mom said.

I sighed. "What about Jean and the little girl?" I
asked in a ragged voice.

"We don't know yet. Jean was hurt internally. Go

back to sleep now. The doctor said we can take you home tomorrow, but Tomás will have to stay here a few days."

She bent and kissed my cheek, then sat down beside me. I reached for her hand, held on tight, and closed my eyes.

When I awakened next I saw a dim light coming through the windows. I felt disoriented, but then I realized that I was hungry and thirsty, and that it must be almost morning. I looked around the room and saw another bed with a form in it and heard soft snoring. I hadn't known I had company, but decided being quiet was a good idea. Whoever was in that bed had a reason to be in the hospital, and I didn't want to disturb her.

I stared out the window as the sky lightened, feeling more and more confused. What was I going to say about the accident? The car from behind had hit us, but it certainly wasn't that driver's fault. If Jim hadn't passed him going so fast and then lost control of our car, we wouldn't have been in a spot where the other car could have hit us. Things were a muddle in my mind.

Would the police question me? Should I tell them that Jim had been drinking beer? Could I prove that he had really been drinking beer? He had said it was lemonade, but I'd seen him wiping foam off his mouth. Besides, that cup I picked up hadn't been a lemonade cup.

Suddenly I realized that I hadn't asked anyone about Jim. I had asked about Tomás and Jean, but I hadn't spared a thought for Jim. Then I remembered the lady telling me he was all right.

My thoughts chased themselves around my head while the sun rose. If I told the police Jim had been drinking, would they put him in jail? What would Tomás think of me if I squealed on Jim? A squealer. A person who finks to the cops, I thought bitterly.

Could they put all of us in jail, I wondered. But I hadn't done anything. "Yes, you did," I argued back with myself. "You got into that car. Mistake *numero uno.*"

My head was aching by this time, and my stomach howled for food and I had to go to the bathroom. Where were all the nurses and doctors who were supposed to hover around the beds of accident victims?

The patient in the other bed was still asleep although daylight flooded the room. I slid out of bed and paddled across the floor in my bare feet and opened the door. Yippee, the bathroom. When I returned to the bed, lurching somewhat lopsidedly because of the weight of the cast, a voice spoke.

"Auto accident, huh?" a girl said in a sleep-fogged

voice. "With me it was an angry appendix."

She was young, and as she sat up in the bed, I could see that she was about twenty-five pounds too heavy. If there is one thing I can't stand it's people who eat too much and get fat. We see plenty of them on the beach at Santo Rosario. They are always the girls who pour themselves into too small bikinis.

"How did it happen?" she asked eagerly. "Anyone killed?"

"It happened too fast for me to know how it happened," I mumbled and pulled the blanket up to my eyes. I didn't want to talk about the accident to anyone, least of all to an obese thrill-seeker.

While I watched, she swung out of bed and started putting on lipstick. Yuck, I thought, without even brushing her teeth. Which reminded me that I didn't have a toothbrush of my own.

All of a sudden, as if to make up for not being around earlier, the hospital routine started with a bustle. There was wash water, breakfast, baths, bed-changing, and a doctor who said my arm would be as good as new in six weeks and that I could go home as soon as my parents arrived.

Behind him came an officer from the highway patrol with questions about the accident. "It happened so fast that I don't really know how it happened," I said, telling myself that I was only skirting the edge of a lie.

"Jean was screaming." I stopped and looked at him. "I wish someone would tell me how Jean is."

"She's in intensive care, but the doctors think she will be all right," he said. "She'll be here for some time, though. I'm told you can go home today. You were lucky."

I nodded. "How about Jim?"

"A couple of bruised ribs, but he'll be fine. He was driving too fast, wasn't he? What was the big hurry?"

Suddenly I was back there on the highway with the fender screeching as it hit the divider. Then I saw the little girl with the blood streaming from her forehead again, and I started to cry.

"You kids were lucky you didn't kill anyone," the officer said.

My mother hurried through the door with an armload of clothes and my shoulder bag. "What's this?" she demanded.

"Just investigating the accident, ma'am," the officer answered.

"Well, go investigate someplace else," she ordered. "My daughter wasn't driving the car, and she's upset enough now."

She helped me dress and checked me out of the hospital. Dad was waiting beside the car, and he held the door open while I settled myself on the back seat. I clenched my teeth when we swung onto the freeway, and I closed my eyes when we reached that curve just below the summit. Mom and Dad helped by chatting about the nice weather and a movie they had seen on television on Saturday night, but my jaws were aching from clenching my teeth when we pulled into the driveway.

Going into the house I was uneasy and wondered what I was going to say when they asked me about the accident. I knew they would ask and wondered what Tomás had told them. If I knew my mother, she would forbid us to have anything more to do with Jim if she heard the whole story. I didn't want that to happen—not yet, anyway. Not while I felt he was a possible suspect.

Dad settled me down in front of the television and said he was going to work. Mom would stay with me the rest of the day, and tomorrow I could go back to school.

Mom tucked a pillow under my cast and asked if I were comfortable. Then she sat down in a chair opposite me, and I feared I was in for a long, difficult session.

"Don't worry. I won't ride with him again," I promised, figuring disarming her before she started with the questions would be a good idea.

"How did it happen?" she asked.

"Tomás told him to slow down, but he didn't," I

explained carefully. "Then we hit the divider." I started to shudder. "I don't want to talk about it; I don't even want to think about it."

"It usually helps to talk about things instead of keeping them bottled up inside," Mom said. "We'll drop it for now, but I will tell you that your father and I had some moments of pure agony when we heard about the accident."

I nodded. I knew she was right, but I didn't want to talk to her because I was afraid I would let something slip about the beer. Mom would explode like a firecracker on a hot stove if she heard about that. I decided to keep my mouth shut until I had a chance to talk to Tomás.

🎗️ 8 🎗️

Tomás came home on Wednesday afternoon. I had spent two miserable days at school, trying to manage books, pencils, and notebook, and open my locker with one hand. It made me angry because I had to keep asking for help. What made me even angrier were the stories floating around school. Stories about Jean being at death's door when in fact she was much better and would be home in a week. Then I heard another story that Jim's careful and skillful driving had kept us all from being killed. I snorted when I heard that and walked away. The only good thing I heard was that Jim would have to appear in traffic court. I hoped the judge would ground him for life.

We had a celebration dinner Wednesday night for Tomás. Mom made chicken *enchiladas* and *frijoles,* and he ate as if his hospital fare had been rationed.

Mom and Dad made a big fuss over Tomás, but they didn't talk about the accident. Maybe they had covered the subject during the ride home from the hospital. Anyway, it was almost time for bed before I had a chance to talk to Tomás alone. He had walked around the house as if he were seeing it with new eyes. I knew the feeling. The first night I had been home I fingered all my books and then dragged a dilapidated teddy bear from the chest at the foot of my bed. I had gone to sleep with him on my pillow.

Mom and Dad finally turned on the television, and Tomás went to his room. He was lying on the bed, staring at the ceiling, when I tapped on the half-opened door.

"I'm glad my head has stopped aching," he said. "I'll have to hit the books hard starting tomorrow to catch up."

I nodded sympathetically. "Did that highway patrolman come and question you?" I asked in a whisper.

Tomás motioned me to close the door, even though the television was plenty loud. "*Si,*" he answered and continued in Spanish. "He asked all kinds of questions. How fast did I think Jim was going? Why were we going so fast? Had we been drinking? And on and on. Those guys never give up."

"What did you tell him?"

"I told him the truth—that I'd told Jim to slow

66

down, and that I hadn't been drinking. What did you say?"

"Just that it happened so fast that I didn't really know how it did happen, and then, dumb me, I started to cry. I feel like crying yet when I think about it."

Tomás looked troubled. "Did you say anything about Jim's drinking?"

I told him that I hadn't. "I couldn't actually prove it. Besides, I wanted to talk to you first. Say, there's a story floating around school about Jim being a big hero and saving us with his skillful driving."

"I'll bet he started that himself. He's probably hoping the judge will go easy on him in traffic court."

"Why do you let that character hang around?"

Tomás eased another pillow under his head. "I've really felt sorry for him. In fact, I still do. Jim and his father drove over to the hospital last night. Jim's all shook up about the accident. He sort of choked out an apology. And that father of his! Talk about mean. He acted as if Jim had committed the crime of the century."

"He *was* driving too fast, and he *had* been drinking," I insisted.

"You don't like him, Nancy. Why did you keep quiet about it?"

"Mom would never allow either of us to have anything to do with him if she knew about the beer. You know that. So I kept quiet because I figured you'd better stay pals with him. I still think it odd that the station-wagon people packed up and left right after he talked to them."

Then I remembered that I hadn't had a chance to explain things to Tomás before Jim had come up and interrupted with the belt. "You know, the station-wagon people that the Olssens told us about. I saw Jim talking to them just before they left the flea market. Maybe he's connected with them. Maybe he was in on the robbery."

"Don't be an idiot, Nancy. Jim wouldn't do a thing like that. He just *couldn't* be part of it. I know he seems to have an awful lot of money to spend. But wouldn't he have warned them not to come to the flea market? He's a smart guy."

"I thought of that, too," I admitted. "Still, I saw him talking to those people and they *did* have Grandfather's belts."

Tomás fiddled with his pillow. "I just can't believe Jim could be involved. What we'd better do is go see the Olssens tomorrow after school and find out if they know anything more about the station-wagon people."

"How can we be certain the Olssens are innocent? Maybe they are part of a gang. They could be selling stolen goods for the crooks. We only have their word that they bought the belts from the station-wagon couple." I hated to voice my suspicions of that sweet-faced old lady, but the possibility of their being involved nibbled at the back of my mind.

"Nancy, you can't believe that. They gave us the belts and the money."

"That could have been just to throw us off the track," I argued. "Maybe we should go to the police and tell them the whole story. About Jim's drinking. About the station-wagon people and the afghan I saw, and about the Olssens and the belts. Jim spotted those belts too easily. As if he knew where to find them."

"Your imagination is stampeding. If Jim had known where to find the belts, do you think he would have led us to them? All he had to do was say he'd checked that row and we would never have seen them."

"Maybe the beer had addled his brains."

Tomás sat up straight. "I wish you'd get off that beer business. Jim's my friend. I know he doesn't booze."

"I know he almost killed us." I was angry and close to tears.

Tomás' voice softened. "I didn't know he could be a wild man behind the wheel, Nancy, or I'd never have suggested that we ride with him. But we can't go to the police. We haven't any evidence. I'm not going to get Jim or a nice old couple like the Olssens into

69

trouble because of your crazy suspicions."

"We have the belts. The Olssens had the belts. That's not suspicion. That's fact."

"Agreed." Tomás was silent for a long moment. He pulled off his headband and stared at it. "I wonder what an Apache chief would do if his friend . . . "

Suddenly I felt sorry for Tomás. I knew the fierce loyalties he developed for his friends and I knew how awful I would feel if we were talking about Jean instead of Jim. "Why don't we follow our original plan?" I suggested. "Go see the Olssens tomorrow. Maybe we'll get a chance to look around their house. You can always ask for a drink of water or something."

"Play super sleuth." Tomás' face brightened. "We'll soon find out what kind of people they are."

"You meet me at Jake's Hamburger Joint. I'll call Grandmother before I leave for school in the morning and tell her we'll be late."

9

Well, of course Mom heard me on the phone. First to Mrs. Olssen explaining why we hadn't shown up on Monday and asking if we could come this afternoon, and then to Grandmother. "Who are these Olssens?" she asked as she drove me to school.

"They're a nice old couple we met at the flea market," I evaded, deciding not to tell her anything about the belts or the station-wagon couple. "They do a lot of selling there and they offered to help us price our things for the garage sale."

"Now don't you go bothering those people."

"Oh, Mom, we're not. Mrs. Olssen volunteered. She's neat, like Grandmother. Besides, she knows a lot about antiques."

"I didn't realize you were interested in antiques."

"I'm not really. Just curious." I started to tell her

about the incident at the "Blue Pelican." Just then we pulled up in front of my school and I scrambled out of the car, glad to get away from her questions.

I waved at my mother and walked toward my locker. I didn't have many close friends and I missed Jean terribly. Without her, I had no one to share secrets with. I still shook when I thought about how close she had come to being killed.

Robin Watson was standing next to my locker when I reached it, and she offered to hold my books. It was nice of her, but the real reason popped out when she asked me how Tomás was. I'd probably have loads of friends in high school next year, all of them wanting to get close to Tomás' sister.

The day slid by in haphazard fashion. One of those days during which nothing really goes wrong, but not a day you would want to paste in your memory book, either.

I skipped lunch and only had a candy bar from the vending machine so I would have enough money for a chocolate soda when I reached Jake's. It's a funny little lunch counter, but we like it because Jake likes us. Down the street at Crushin's Restaurant, they are always telling us to hurry up and get out of the booths, but Jake doesn't mind if we sit and talk. So I perched on a stool and slowly worked on my soda while Jake fried onions to go with a hamburger someone had ordered. That's another thing that Jake does. Ever had fried onions on your hamburger? Most places won't bother with them, but at Jake's they are a house specialty.

I was wondering if I'd recognize the station-wagon girl if I saw her again when Tomás and Pete Higgins arrived. I saw, with relief, that Jim Block wasn't along. I slid off the stool, and the three of us started down the street. The address given us by the Olssens was on Rose Street, about six blocks from Grandmother's. It was in an older part of town where small houses hid behind overgrown shrubbery. I noted that a lot of the houses needed paint and said so to Tomás.

"Paint costs money," Tomás replied. "Just like the new roof Grandfather needs. I'll bet most of these people are on Social Security and don't have much extra to spend."

The Olssens' small house didn't need paint. Its white coat sparkled in the sun and the blue trim around the windows was just the right touch for the old Victorian cottage.

Mr. Olssen answered the door and invited us inside. The small living room, furnished with only a sofa, chair, television, and a few tables and lamps, was uncluttered, but the dining room behind it looked like a store. The table and buffet were covered with glassware, vases, and dishes. Boxes sat under the table and on the chairs. A stack of picture frames leaned against the wall.

Mrs. Olssen bustled in from the kitchen with a plate of cookies in her hand. "Lucky I baked this morning," she said. "I recognized Tomás' voice and he sounds hungry."

She smiled at the boys and gestured at the sofa. Tomás and Pete glanced awkwardly at each other, so I plunged in with an abrupt question. "Your dining room looks like a store. Why is that?" The question sounded rude and I added an apology.

"I guess you could call it a warehouse," Mrs. Olssen said with an understanding smile. "This is such a small place, only one bedroom and a single garage, that we use the dining room for storage."

"But where do you get the things?" Somehow I found it easy to talk to Mrs. Olssen.

"We buy at garage and moving sales and resell at the flea market," Mr. Olssen explained.

Suddenly I remembered where I had seen them before. They had been at several of the garage sales we checked last week. But the Olssens hadn't acted like the gloating, whispering woman. It just wasn't possible that such a nice old couple could be tied up with a gang of thieves, I decided with relief.

Tomás looked at the dining room with interest. "Do

you make any money, and how did you get started doing this?"

"That's an awfully personal question," I protested, feeling my face turn hot.

"We don't mind," Mrs. Olssen said with a smile directed toward her husband. "After we retired, we found life rather dull so it started first as a kind of hobby. We didn't know anyone in Santo Rosario when we moved here and going to garage sales was an excuse to get out of the house. At first we just bought pretty things for our own use. Then I discovered that many people were selling things of value at dime-store prices. About that time inflation hit us, and we started reselling."

Pete stood up and wandered into the dining room. "Looks like a lot of junk to me."

Mr. Olssen laughed. "What's junk to one person is a collector's item to another."

"What we really want to know is if you ever saw the station-wagon people before," I said, leaning forward so I could support my cast on my knee.

"Well, we only go to the Los Olivos flea market about every other month," Mr. Olssen answered, shaking his head. "Generally I walk around while the sellers are setting up to check on prices, and I keep an eye out for any Rookwood we can afford because Iris, here, collects it."

My ears perked up. There was that word "Rook-wood" again, but I didn't ask about it. It was getting late, and we would have to leave soon. "What about the station-wagon people?" I repeated.

"From the description, I believe I've seen them somewhere, but not at the flea market," Mrs. Olssen said.

"Do you think they live here in Santo Rosario?" Tomás asked.

"I just can't remember where I saw them," she answered.

"The boy who was with us is Jim Block. He's the one who bought the belt from you. Have you ever seen him before?" Tomás asked to my surprise. I knew it was painful for him to suggest, even by a question, that Jim might be involved.

"Yes, I think so." Mrs. Olssen turned toward her husband. "Olaf, remember that day, about two weeks ago, when we went to the boardwalk?" Her voice was suddenly excited. "That's where we saw them! They were with a group. Remember why we noticed them? They were drinking from cans wrapped in paper napkins and making loud remarks at everyone who passed. And Jim Block stopped to talk to them. We like to go to the boardwalk occasionally because it's such a happy place," she finished.

Tomás looked as if the weight of the world had descended upon his shoulders. "It could be a mistake," he muttered. "I can't imagine Jim stealing from a bunch of old people. I can't understand why he would do it. His folks bought a large house when they moved here, and his father must have a good job. They have two new cars."

"He's not really so nice," I said. That remark about the doll buggy still rankled and so did the accident.

"There's one way to find out," Pete suggested. "We can hang around the boardwalk. Maybe we can spot Jim talking to those people."

"I have been thinking that I should tell the police about buying the belts from the couple with the station wagon," Mr. Olssen said in a troubled voice. "Iris disagrees with me. She says they could be innocent."

Mrs. Olssen's short white hair bounced as she nodded vigorously. "That's right. It's possible they bought those belts from someone else."

Depression, as heavy as the cast on my arm, settled over me. The station-wagon people were the only lead we had, but I realized she could be right. "We have to leave now," I said. "Can we come back tomorrow? I want to find out about the Rookwood."

She nodded and I remembered to thank her for the cookies. Pete started for home and we hurried toward

Grandmother's house, Tomás muttering savagely to himself. I kept quiet. I liked Mrs. Olssen. I didn't want to point out that her identification of the station-wagon pair, when she hadn't even seen them at the flea market, as people that Jim knew, could be a way of diverting our attention from her and her husband.

Her suggestion that the couple might be innocent only increased my suspicions. I could see no reason for them to have left the flea market so hurriedly and with so much unsold merchandise—no reason at all unless Jim had warned them.

𝔢❖𝔢 **10** 𝔢❖𝔢

I stopped outside the front door. "Tomás, those belts are still in my shoulder bag and you have the money the Olssens gave you. Shouldn't we give it to the grandparents?"

"You keep that purse of yours and your mouth shut, Nancy!" Tomás snapped. "If we give Grandfather the belts and money, we'll have to explain how we got them. They'll either call the police or talk things over with the parents. Then we'll be in for it. Just keep quiet."

"But the grandparents need the money."

"We'll give it to them after we track down those crooks. Then the Olssens will be in the clear."

I agreed and we went into the house.

Grandmother made a big fuss over Tomás. She had *empanadas* and a tall glass of milk waiting for him.

Frankly, I felt that with my broken arm I should be considered more of an invalid than Tomás, who didn't even have a headache now, but that wasn't the case.

"*Madre de Dios,*" she prayed, bustling around the kitchen. "Sit down and give your poor head a rest, Tomás."

I looked at my brother wolfing down the meat-filled *empanadas* and lapping up the attention as if he were an Arabian prince in a harem. "You'll never be able to eat dinner," I said. "Especially after all of Mrs. Olssen's cookies and now these *empanadas.*"

"Don't fuss at your brother, Nancy," my grandmother ordered. "He's a growing boy and he needs to eat to keep up his strength after that dreadful accident." She beamed at Tomás, settled into her rocker, and picked up her crocheting.

"Oh, good," I said. "You're crocheting again."

"Our Social Security checks came yesterday. Your grandfather bought more leather and I bought yarn." Grandmother looked troubled, but determined. "We'll work hard to add to the roof fund."

"We'll pray for a dry winter," Grandfather added. "Maybe we can manage until next year by putting some buckets in the attic."

Depression settled even deeper as I thought of the storms that whipped in from the southwest during the winter. Last year the heavy clouds had brought forty-three inches of rain to Santo Rosario. It had rained and rained and rained. They had used so many kettles under the leaks they had none left to cook in. If the weather was that bad again this winter, they'd need more than buckets in the attic.

Attic! Suddenly I sat straight up and stared at Grandmother, remembering the rainy days we had spent in the attic when we were younger. Why, that attic was a storehouse of treasures! There were barrels and boxes and trunks filled with clothes, dishes, photograph albums, books, and linens. There was old furniture, and even toys. Grandmother never threw out anything. All of her mother's things were stored up there and all those of her great-aunt, Maria Sanchez, who had died last year, and there were generations of Pérez belongings. Why, we could have the grandmother and grandfather of garage sales! I started to say so, then decided to keep quiet for the time being. My grandmother had a lot of old things, things that might be considered antiques. I knew I needed to find out more about antiques before I made any suggestions.

I spread out my books on the kitchen table and started my homework to the sound of Grandmother's rocker creaking back and forth. Tomás wandered to the basement where Grandfather had gone to work on his belts. "We'll be late again tomorrow," I said. "We're going to the Olssens' after school."

"Again?" Grandmother's voice sounded funny. "Are her cookies better than mine?"

I went over and gave her a kiss. "No one makes better cookies than you, but Mrs. Olssen promised to teach me something about antiques. You should see her dining room. It looks like a store."

Grandmother nodded. "So does mine. That china cabinet is so cluttered that you can't even see what is in it. I think I'll sort out some of the junk and get rid of it."

I gasped. "No, don't! That would spoil all my plans."

"What plans?"

Well, I'd done it. "I wasn't going to tell you yet, but I guess I'd better. I was thinking about the attic and all the old things up there. You know, *Abuelita*, you could have a king-sized garage sale and make a lot of money."

"Who'd pay out good money for that old junk?"

"It's not junk. You should see the prices they ask at the flea market for what are called 'collectibles.' "

Grandmother looked at me thoughtfully. "It's not a bad idea," she said. "We really need that roof before the rains start. I'll talk to your grandfather and see what he says. You learn what you can from Mrs. Olssen."

"I'll try," I promised and turned back to my algebra.

At dinner, after we were home, Tomás brought up the subject of our going to the boardwalk on Saturday night. I think he figured asking a couple of days ahead would give the parents a chance to get used to the idea.

Dad shook his head. "You know how we feel about kids being out after dark unsupervised."

"Dad, the boardwalk isn't dark. There are bright lights from beginning to end," Tomás protested.

I had a sudden inspiration. "Mom, one of the themes Mrs. Bunton assigned has to be about Santo Rosario. I've decided to write about the boardwalk. You know how pretty it is at night, with the lights on the rides glittering. Tomás said he'd take me. Please let us go." I flashed my brother a warning look, hoping he'd go along with my story. I wasn't exactly lying. Mrs. Bunton *had* told us one theme must be about Santo Rosario, and I made up my mind right then to write about the boardwalk.

"You've been to the boardwalk dozens of times," Mom said, a frown on her face. "Surely you remember enough about it to write a theme."

"Mom, the boardwalk is mostly for tourists. We haven't been there in years," I protested.

Mom's face softened. "I guess, since Tomás will be with you and it's for a school project, we should consider letting you go."

"We're not babies," Tomás said. "You know I'll take

care of Nancy. I promise I won't let her out of my sight."

"All right," Dad agreed. "You may go. I'll pick you up at the merry-go-round at nine o'clock. That's plenty late enough."

"What about this famous garage sale of yours?" Mom asked. "I was looking forward to a cleaned-out closet."

"We're sort of waiting for Jean to come home," I said. "She'll be out of the hospital Saturday. She told me so when I talked to her on the phone."

"There's not enough time this week," Tomás added. "We'll get it in the paper next week."

"You had better not wait much longer. We're having a dry autumn, but it's certain to rain soon," Dad said.

Gloom settled over all of us. I knew my father had offered Grandfather the money for a new roof and had been refused. I'd heard Dad muttering to Mom about stiff-necked, stupid, Spanish pride. "You'd think he was *un grande de España.*"

"The old need their pride," Mom had answered.

That remark popped back into my head as I gathered up my books and went to my room. How old were Grandmother and Grandfather? Funny, I'd never thought of them as old before. They'd just always been there—my grandparents—my only grandparents because my mother's parents had died before I was born.

I sat down on my bed and started figuring. I knew my mother had been thirty when I was born. That made her forty-three now, and my father was seven years older than she was. Wow, Dad was fifty! Why, they were *old*.

If my father was fifty, then my grandfather must be seventy or even older. I shivered. Seventy was awfully old. I tried to think of myself as seventy, but trying to imagine all those years made my head ache. Why, it was an eternity just to the end of the school year.

That reminded me of the essay on Thoreau. Mrs. Bunton had bounced it back at me with an order to rewrite it. "Sloppy, poorly organized, and shows no thinking," were her comments. It was a dumb assignment, anyway. If Thoreau were alive today, he wouldn't be Thoreau. I sighed and opened my notebook.

༄༅ 11 ༄༅

Tomás and I went to the Olssens' house after school the next day, and Mrs. Olssen tried to cram some knowledge of antiques into my head while Tomás stuffed himself with cookies. He especially liked the small ones shaped like an *S* which she said were Swedish cookies called *spritz baklese*.

We left convinced that the Olssens were completely honest. "No one who makes cookies as good as she does could be a thief," Tomás declared.

I agreed with him. Mrs. Olssen was kind and generous with her time and knowledge. Mr. Olssen worked hard repairing and refinishing antique furniture which they'd bought to resell. Crooks didn't act like that.

When we reached our grandparents' house, Grandmother had a plate of *churros*, lemon-flavored crullers, waiting. It seemed almost as if the two ladies were having a contest to see who could put the most pounds on Tomás' bones.

On Saturday morning we hurried through our weekly chores. Tomás mowed the lawn and trimmed shrubs while I weeded the flower beds. I dusted the furniture and mopped the kitchen floor, doing a very sloppy one-handed job. Tomás vacuumed and put clothes into the washer and dryer.

When the work was done, we went to my room and started putting price stickers on the toys and games. I told Tomás about my idea of Grandmother's having a garage sale with all the old things packed away in her attic.

"She could call it an attic sale," he suggested. "You know, maybe we could combine our garage sale with theirs. That would save money on advertising. Why don't we go over there and plan it with them? It's too early to go to the boardwalk, anyway."

I dug out the price guide to antiques that Mrs. Olssen had loaned me, and we walked over to our grandparents' house. It would have been faster to take our bikes, but Mom had warned me that I wasn't to touch mine until my cast was removed.

Grandmother was frosting a chocolate cake when we entered the kitchen, and Tomás' hug was extra hearty as he greeted her.

"You must have smelled it all the way over at our house," I said to him. "Between the goodies at Mrs. Olssen's and here, I'll bet you've gained five pounds in the last three days."

"Stop nagging your brother," Grandmother said. "He shot up like a beanpole this last summer and he needs some fat on those bones."

"Did you ask Grandfather about the garage sale?" I asked.

"We talked it over. He said I could sell whatever I choose, but there are some things I'm going to save. Heirlooms that I want to give you and Tomás when you get married," she replied.

"Married! *Ugh*. That's years and years away," Tomás said. "Where's Grandfather?"

"In the basement sorting out tools. He told me he had many duplicates he doesn't need. Maybe he'll find some to sell."

"Guess I'll see if I can help him. Be sure to call me when you are ready to cut that cake." Tomás clattered down the steps to the basement while I watched Grandmother swirl on the last of the frosting.

"What's up in the attic that could be called heirlooms?" I asked.

"Well, Haviland china for a start. Both my mother and Great-aunt Maria had complete sets. I have Mother Pérez' set myself, so I thought I'd give each of you a set of Haviland. I'm not certain just what is packed in the barrels, but I think there is some crystal."

I gasped. From reading the antique price guide I knew that a set of Haviland could be worth several hundred dollars. "Tomás and I wondered if we could combine our garage sale with yours. We could bring our things over here, and it would save money on advertising and be more fun."

"How would we keep the money separate?"

"Why would we need to? It all goes into the roof fund."

Grandmother's face closed up in stiff, proud lines. "We can't let you do that. The roof is our problem."

I was almost in tears. Somehow I thought they had understood when we first talked about having a garage sale, when we'd asked if Grandfather would supervise. "But you *have* to," I protested. "That's what we planned it for after the Co-op was robbed. We are selling things we never use. Toys and games we're tired of and all those outgrown clothes that are jammed into my closet. Nothing that we want to keep."

"Still, they belong to you, and surely you could find some place to spend the money. Your grandfather wouldn't allow it." Grandmother's eyes flashed and she drew herself up as if she were trying to stretch her five feet to six. "We won't argue about it. Let's go up to the attic and see what's there."

I thought furiously while I followed her up the two flights of stairs. Sure I could use the money. Maybe Mr. Jackson would make me another silver bracelet like the stolen one if I could pay for it. But the whole point of our sale was to help with the roof fund. I had to find some way to convince them. Maybe Tomás would come up with an answer when I talked to him.

Grandmother snapped on the attic light. "I haven't been up here in years except to sweep down the cobwebs and dust the floor. I'm not really certain what is packed in the trunks."

"There are lots of your old clothes. I think one trunk is full of velvet jackets with braid on them and long skirts and silky short dresses with fringes," I said, remembering the fun Jean and I used to have dressing up in them. I wished Jean were here instead of in the hospital. She'd love to help unpack the trunks.

"The old clothes are nothing but junk," Grandmother said. "We'll leave them for the last." She went to the first trunk, opened it, and removed a layer of newspaper. I'd never been interested in most of the trunks because they were piled full of linens. Grandmother lifted out a stack of pillow cases and put them on the newspaper. "Great-aunt Maria prided herself on her embroidery," she said. "Her linens were beautiful."

There were stacks of tablecloths, dresser scarves, and sheets, all heavily embroidered. Some were edged with a kind of lace I'd never seen. Grandmother called it "Battenberg."

"Why don't you use these pretty pillow cases?" I asked, looking at one with a band of roses embroidered across the end.

"Too much work ironing them," she answered. "I much prefer permanent press." She was holding a bulky object swathed in a bath towel. "Let's see what we have here."

She unwrapped a large bowl on a pedestal. "It's a compote," she explained. "Great-aunt Maria always had it on her sideboard filled with fruit."

I took the white dish which was trimmed with a gold tea-leaf pattern and turned it over. On the bottom it said "Burgess, Burselm" and there was a funny mark.

"I think this is ironstone," I said. "It looks like a piece of ironstone Mrs. Olssen showed me." I set it on the floor and started looking in the price guide. "Here it is," I said, my voice going high with excitement. "Six-inch compote. One hundred twenty-five dollars."

Grandmother stared at me. "That can't be right.

Great-aunt Maria never paid anything like that for it."

I handed her the book. "Look for yourself."

"I think there are more pieces with the same tea-leaf pattern." She unwrapped a pitcher and a soup tureen with a cover.

I studied the price guide and shook my head. "I just wouldn't know what prices to put on things like these. Why don't we ask Mrs. Olssen to help us?"

That closed look returned to Grandmother's face. "We'd have to pay her, and the purpose of the sale is to make money for the roof fund, not spend it."

"Mrs. Olssen isn't that kind of person," I protested. "She'd probably get mad if you offered to pay her."

"You know what your grandfather would say." She clipped off the words.

"I don't know why you won't let someone help who knows what she is doing! *You're* always helping other people. Look what you do for Tomás and me," I argued.

"That's different. You two are my family."

"Then you should let us have our garage sale here and take the money for the roof fund. You're *our* family," I said, glad to find a loophole in her reasoning.

She sighed. "Maybe you have a point there, but I don't think your grandfather will agree."

"You could let me ask Mrs. Olssen to help us, but I don't think she'd do it for money. Maybe you could give her a present," I suggested, looking at two vases she'd found near the bottom of the trunk. They were a pair, about ten inches high, decorated with pink and white flowers. I turned one over and discovered it was marked "Nippon." "These things are *really* collectible, and I just don't know how to price them."

Grandmother found a box, and we put the carefully wrapped ironstone and vases into it. "Let's take these downstairs. I'll heat up some soup for lunch, and we'll talk to your grandfather."

While Grandmother bustled about her kitchen, I looked up Nippon in the price guide. The vases were listed at thirty-five to sixty dollars. It didn't say if a pair was worth more, and I wondered how to find out because none of the vases described were similar to Grandmother's.

In a few moments the soup was steaming. Tomás and Grandfather came up from the basement, and we started to eat. "Grandfather has tons of extra tools he can sell," Tomás announced.

"That's because I had tools and my father had tools," Grandfather explained.

"Sounds as if you've been saving things, too," Grandmother said with a smile. "For years you've accused me of turning the attic into a junk shop. Maybe now you'll be glad I did."

"I still can't understand why you hung onto all

those dinky books of Juan's. You could have tossed them out when he married."

I grabbed for the price guide. I had forgotten about the huge box filled with Big Little Books that Tomás and I had read and reread during rainy afternoons. There had been Little Orphan Annie and Dick Tracy and Mickey Mouse. And several books about Tailspin Tommy. I had flipped over Tailspin Tommy and his daring adventures when I was nine. "Here it is," I yelled. "Big Little Books, priced at three to ten dollars each. There's a whole box of them in the attic!"

"They belong to your father," Grandfather said. "We can't sell his books without his permission, and if he gave it, we would turn over the money to him."

"Oh, Grandfather," I said, exasperated. "You and Grandmother are just impossible. Father would *want* you to have the money. You know that. Grandmother won't let me ask Mrs. Olssen to help price the antiques without paying her, and I just know Mrs. Olssen won't accept money. Wouldn't you even let me ask her over to *look* at the things? I know you would like her, and they don't have many friends in Santo Rosario. They haven't lived here long, and you would be doing *them* a favor."

Grandfather sat erect at the head of the table. "Your grandmother and I will discuss the matter, but we do not sell other people's property. That is dishonest."

94

I looked at Tomás in dismay. He winked at me and then turned to Grandfather. "The Olssens have been of much help to Nancy and me, and they have been extremely hospitable. It's embarrassing when we can't invite them to our house, but you know Mom and Dad like to have quiet Sundays," he said in a formal tone most unlike him.

Grandfather unbent a trifle. "If that is the case, you could invite them here Monday after school."

Grandmother smiled. "I'll make a flan and a special coconut cake. Poor lady, no wonder she's making such a fuss with her cookies. She must be terribly lonely. Call her right now, Nancy."

I met Tomás' smile with some misgivings. He'd managed the situation with guile, but I wasn't exactly easy in my mind. The Olssens didn't expect us to return their hospitality and it seemed to me that they led busy, happy lives, but I kept quiet. Sometimes it's best to let adults delude themselves.

❦❦ **12** ❦❦

Tomás and I left our grandparents' house late in the afternoon and started toward the boardwalk. At the end of the block I stopped and grabbed Tomás' arm. "We have to talk to the Olssens right away!"

"What for?"

"The belts."

Tomás' face looked as dismayed as I felt. We turned the corner and hurried the half mile to the Olssens' white Victorian cottage and rang the bell.

Mrs. Olssen appeared surprised as she opened the door. "I didn't think I'd see you this soon after talking to you on the telephone, Nancy. It's kind of your grandparents to invite us to their home. I'm looking forward to meeting them."

"That's what we want to talk to you about," Tomás said.

The welcoming smile faded from Mrs. Olssen's face as she motioned us into the living room. Mr. Olssen turned off the football game he'd been watching on television and looked at us.

I shifted my weight from one foot to the other, wondering what to say. "It's about the belts," I blurted.

Mr. Olssen frowned. "We gave you the belts and the money."

"You don't understand. I have the money and Nancy has the belts in her purse. You see, if we gave the belts and money to our grandparents, we'd have to tell them the whole thing about the station-wagon people. We're afraid the grandparents would go to the police," Tomás explained.

"Maybe *you* should go to the police," Mr. Olssen answered in a stern voice. "Maybe we all should."

"We don't know who those station-wagon people are. Nancy didn't get the license number. All we know is that Jim Block was talking to them and you bought some of Grandfather's belts from them. We don't want to get anyone in trouble," Tomás argued.

"We have nothing to hide," Mrs. Olssen said proudly. "But it is possible that this station-wagon pair are as innocent as we are." She smiled gently at her husband. "Olaf, remember how crushed we all were when Lars was unfairly accused of stealing money out of a neighbor's house? Lars was our son. He was nine then. He didn't come back from Korea," she explained to us.

I swallowed hard. "But—"

Tomás interrupted. "Jim is my friend. He's in a lot of trouble already. He lost his license because of the accident and his father says he can't drive until he can buy a car of his own. He says his parents will hardly talk to him. I just can't believe Jim could be involved in the robbery and I don't want to cause more trouble for him."

Mr. Olssen studied Tomás' face for a long moment. "What will you do if you discover that your friend is connected with a gang of thieves that prey on old people—your own grandparents?" he asked.

Tomás flinched. "I-I just don't know."

"We really don't believe he is," I said, feeling so sorry for my brother that I wanted to cry. "Please don't tell our grandparents about the belts or the station-wagon people yet. Give us a chance to track them down."

The Olssens looked at each other. Mrs. Olssen nodded. "All right," Mr. Olssen said. "But I want you two to promise us that you'll be careful. If those people are crooks, they'll face a stiff jail sentence when they're caught and they could be dangerous."

"We won't go looking for trouble," Tomás agreed. "And thank you, both of you."

We said good-bye and headed toward the board-walk. Tomás was silent as we walked slowly down the street. I kept quiet, realizing that my brother was trying to sort things out. Even though I had told the Olssens differently, I still believed that Jim was involved with those crooks. I was glad that I didn't have to make the difficult decision that I feared Tomás faced.

My cast hampered me and Tomás adjusted to my slower pace as we hiked the mile and a half from the Olssens' house to the beach front. The air was still warm although the sun was close to setting. A faint whisper of a breeze brought the salt tang in from the ocean. I hoped the sunny weather would continue at least until the end of the month. September and October were our best months. July and August, when the tourists crowd our beaches, are usually foggy for at least half the day.

"I wish Jean were here," I said, adjusting the sling which was hurting my neck. "It seems strange to be going places without her, and school's been just rotten."

"I miss her, too," Tomás answered. "She's fun because she laughs a lot. You take things so seriously."

I considered that remark as we continued walking. A part of Jean's charm was her ready laugh, often at herself. "Maybe I should start taking smile lessons," I said.

"You're all right, but you could practice cracking a grin now and then."

"What exactly are we going to do?" I asked as we neared the arcade.

"Look for Jim and those people you saw him talking to at the flea market."

"But what do we do if we find them?"

"Play it by ear. Follow them if we can. Or try to get the license number of their car."

"It's going to be hard to be friendly toward Jim, but I guess we have to be," I said. "We don't want him to think we suspect him."

"You're jumping to conclusions again. We still don't *know* that he's part of a gang of thieves, and he's still my friend," Tomás reminded me.

You might have known it would be Jim who saw us first. He was lounging against the wall near the entrance to the arcade. "Well, look who's here," he called to us. "How did you two manage to get out by yourselves?"

"The parents are relaxing the rules a bit, especially as we and they get older," Tomás answered easily.

"Now that you're out of the house, what about joining a bunch of us up at Two Mile Beach tonight? We're going to have a bonfire and a few bottles of *vino*. I'm afraid it will be a bit much for little sister, but you're welcome to come, Tomás."

Little sister, indeed. I started to sputter, but Tomás cut me off. "I'm afraid the rules aren't that relaxed, Jim. Dad is picking us up later," he said.

A funny look, it seemed to me almost one of envy, crossed Jim's face. "Still an apron-strings boy, huh, Tomás?" he jeered and sauntered into the arcade.

"Now what?" I asked.

"We'll follow him and try to stay out of sight," Tomás said. "If only I could go to that party! I'll bet I could find out plenty there."

"How does he get wine and where does he find the money?"

Tomás shook his head sadly. "Maybe you were right about the drinking. He told me once he got fifteen bucks a week allowance which included lunch money. That would leave plenty for wine. And buying it is no problem. There are always older guys who'll get it for you."

We moved slowly into the arcade where rows of machines waited to gobble up dimes and quarters from people who liked pulling levers. The light was dim, and we paused a few moments near an old slot machine in the form of an Indian chief to allow our eyes to adjust.

"Better get your Indian blood to working," I teased Tomás. "I don't see him."

Tomás peered around the corner of a pillar. "There he is." While we watched, Jim moved desultorily from machine to machine, feeding in coins here and there as he meandered down the left side of the arcade. "Let's start around the other way. Then it won't look like we're following him," Tomás said.

I watched the people carefully as we turned to the

right. We had reached the far wall when I jumped
back, bumping into Tomás. "There, by the baseball
machine. That's the girl. I'm certain of it."

I knew I was right because of the color of her hair.
She wore it in the same heavy braids, this time tied
with green yarn. She hadn't seen me.

Tomás bent over a pinball machine and motioned

me to one side of it. "Pretend you're watching me play. That way you can keep an eye on her. Do you see Jim?"

"No. No sign of him yet."

We were talking in low voices. There weren't too many people inside the arcade and it was kind of spooky with the old-time machines standing about. Then my eyes widened. Jim must have reversed direction. He was coming toward us rapidly.

"*Aquí viene el enemigo,*" I whispered.

Tomás was concentrating on the pinball machine and didn't answer.

"I'm tired of this spooky place," I said in a loud voice and grabbed my brother's arm, pulling him around. "Come on. You said we'd ride the bumper cars."

"What?" Tomás jumped. Then he saw Jim. "Okay, Nancy, we'll do the bumper cars, but first I want a snowcone." He gave Jim a casual wave as we headed toward the door.

We settled down on a bench opposite the arcade with our snowcones and waited. "She could go out the other door," I said, keeping to Spanish. It seemed odd to me that Jim had started down one side of the room, then reversed his course, as if he wanted to make certain he wasn't being watched, and I told Tomás that.

"We can't be sure he was meeting that girl," Tomás

objected, but he spoke in Spanish, too.

"We know he was seen with her once before. It's too much for coincidence," I said.

I looked across the beach at the water. Two sailboats headed for the entrance of the small-craft harbor. "That's what I'd like to have. I wish we could talk the parents into buying a boat."

"They wouldn't have much time for sailing."

I nodded and turned my head back to watch the people passing by. The boardwalk was getting crowded. Tourists wearing loud nautical shirts mingled with jeans-clad students from the university up on the hill. I saw thin girls in long skirts and fat girls in tight pants. Then I saw Jim come out of the arcade alone. "Make your snowcone last," I advised. "Here he comes again. You'd think he was following *us.*"

Tomás' face darkened. "You might be right at that. Maybe he's afraid we saw the girl," he said in Spanish.

Jim came right up to us. "Thought you were headed for the bumper cars," he said.

"Snowcones first," Tomás answered. "You ought to try one."

Jim sat down beside us. He looked at me, at the cast on my arm, then down at his shoes. "Nancy, I'm sorry. I wish it had been my arm instead of yours," he mumbled.

"So do I! And what about Jean?" I snapped.

His face reddened. "I'm awfully sorry about Jean."

"A lot of good that does. You should have laid off the beer," I said.

"A couple of beers doesn't hurt anyone."

Tomás looked straight at Jim. "Your driving landed three of us in the hospital. Why don't you cut out the beer and wine? Who needs it, anyway?"

Jim's face looked troubled. He opened his mouth and started to say something, then shook his head. We finished our snowcones and started for the bumper cars. Jim tagged along and bought himself a ticket.

I wondered what Mom would say if she could see me trying to steer a bumper car one-handed, and after a few minutes I realized I had made a mistake. Jim kept ramming my car and laughing when I tried to stay away from him.

When Tomás saw what was happening, he wheeled his car over and slammed into Jim's. "Keep away from Nancy!" he shouted.

"What's the matter?" Jim yelled. "I'm just trying to give baby sister a thrill."

The ride ended, and I scrambled out of my car. So did Tomás. He walked up to Jim and called him a no good bum who was tied up with a gang of thieves who robbed old people living on pensions, but in *Spanish*.

"Come on," I said and grabbed his arm and pulled

him away before he could switch to English. "Let's get a hot dog."

"You're going to be fat as a cow, little sister," Jim said and doubled up with laughter.

I smiled sweetly and called him a black-tailed jackal in Spanish and we walked away. There are definite advantages to being bilingual. Tomás and I don't generally do this. It is rude, but this time I didn't care.

As we left I noticed a dark-haired young man whom I judged to be a college student grinning at me. *"Bueno,"* he said.

We bought hot dogs, sat down on a bench, and tried to decide what to do next.

"What a stupid thing to say. You'd better not do it again," I warned.

Tomás laughed. "Good thing I was thinking in Spanish."

"Is he still around?" I asked.

"Yep. Over there. Leaning against the fence in front of the Big Dipper."

"I can't believe that he can really suspect we're on to him. After all, almost everyone comes to the boardwalk," I said as I turned to look at Jim.

"Maybe he has a guilty conscience," Tomás suggested, regret in his voice. "If he took part in the robbery, he could be hearing heavy footsteps behind him, especially since he knows we are trying to find the stolen goods."

"Now I know we're right!" I said, grabbing Tomás' arm. "There's the man who was with the girl at the flea market."

He had walked right past us and drifted over to Jim, who was still leaning on the fence.

"We'll follow him," Tomás said.

I had a better idea than that. I jumped up and ran straight over to Jim, who was busy talking to the scrawny-faced man.

"Who's your friend, Jim?" I asked in a honeyed voice, trying to imitate Jean when she was practicing ingenue roles. I directed a smile at the station-wagon man.

"I'm Buck Seymour," he answered before Jim could say a word. Then he sort of leered. "Are you coming to Two Mile Beach, babe? I'll see that you have a good time."

"No, she's not," Jim snapped. "She's a kid. Leave her alone." He glared at me, and I glared right back. Then he turned away. "Come on, Buck," he said. "Let's get away from here and go have some fun."

"See ya around, babe," Buck said and flapped a hand at me.

Buck Seymour, Buck Seymour, I was saying over and over, trying to engrave the name on my memory, when Tomás grabbed my arm and almost shook me.

"What ever did you do that for, you stupid girl?" he demanded in a fierce whisper.

"Don't you call me a stupid girl," I whispered back as I watched Jim and Buck go into the arcade. "He said his name is Buck Seymour. You don't think Jim would have introduced that crook by his right name, do you?"

Tomás released my arm. "Sometime, Nancy, you're going to get yourself into something you can't handle. That guy looked pretty mean to me."

"So what?" I said. "You can take care of 'little sister.' The important thing is that we know his name."

"There are thirty-six thousand people in this town, not counting the tourists. What good does knowing that do?"

Tomás is usually swift with ideas, but there are times when he just isn't practical. I shook my head at him. "The telephone book, dimwit."

"Buck is probably a nickname, but there can't be all that many Seymours," Tomás said thoughtfully. "Let's find a phone booth."

"Why not wait until we get home? I'd like to try the Big Dipper, now that our sleuthing is finished."

Tomás looked at his watch. "We still have time. But remember, Nancy, just because Jim is mixed up with the people who sold Grandfather's belts to the Olssens doesn't mean that he helped rob the Co-op."

"All right, Tomás. He's innocent until proven guilty, but he's a mean, nasty character."

The troubled look returned to Tomás' face. "He's having a hard time getting along at school because he has a know-it-all attitude. Underneath it, he's lonely and he's a nice guy when you get past the shell."

"You must see a side of him I don't, but I'll try to keep an open mind," I promised.

13

As soon as we reached the house, Tomás raced for the telephone book, but Mom stopped me in the living room. "How did your day go?" she asked.

I decided I'd better stay off the subject of Jim Block and his friends. "Mom, I never realized how many treasures *la abuelita* has in her attic. Real antiques. She's going to sell some of them. She had me phone Mrs. Olssen and invite them to her house Monday afternoon. I think she's going to let them help with the pricing. Antiques are neat. When I know more about them, I'm going to start collecting some."

Mom put down her magazine. "I guess I should have known you'd turn out to be an antique buff. Goodness knows, you've exhibited the tendencies of a pack rat since you were three. You must take after your grandmother; you certainly don't get it from me."

I looked around our living room, mentally contrasting it with Grandmother's. A metal sculpture rested on the low blond coffee table. The couch was Danish modern and an abstract painting hung over our fireplace. We had gold wall-to-wall carpeting. Grandmother's rugs were old and faded, but the expanse of floor framing them glistened with wax.

"She said she was going to give me a set of Haviland china when I married," I said.

"You'll have to be very careful when you use it. That's one of the reasons I don't like old things. Off to bed with you now." Mom came over and gave me a kiss and pat on the cheek.

I stopped by Tomás' room. "Eight Seymours and one Seymore," he announced, holding out a list. "But not one of them Buck."

"We might have known it would be a nickname. Now what?"

"I think our best bet is to tie that blue-and-white station wagon you saw to one of these addresses. I guess we'll have to do some real detecting. It sure would help if you could ride a bike."

"We're going to be busy getting ready for the sale," I said. "Don't you think it would be a good idea to lay off a bit?" I shivered, thinking about the glare Jim had given me when I'd learned Buck Seymour's name and Buck's nasty leer. The scrawny-faced man frightened me.

"It sure wouldn't be smart to go back to the board-walk right away. I'll keep my eyes and ears open at school and drop a couple of hints around Jim that we've given up and are concentrating on the garage sale."

"Don't tell him anything about Grandmother's treasures," I warned.

"I'm not that dumb." Tomás stretched and yawned. "Let's get to bed. Detecting is hard work."

In the morning we packed the contents of my toy chest, with the exception of my worn teddy bear, into boxes to take over to our grandparents' house where we were going for dinner.

The food, as usual, was great. We started with pickled tuna.

"Ah, *atún en escabeche. ¡Que delicioso!*" Dad exclaimed as he took a second helping.

"Bill Jackson went fishing a couple of days ago. He shared his catch with us," Grandfather explained.

"I have a pint of it for you to take home," Grandmother told my mother.

"*Gracias,*" Mom said, using one of the few Spanish words she knows. "It'll be a treat. I don't know anyone who cooks as well as you do, and so economically."

"Oh, we have enough money for day-to-day living. It's just hard to save for a big thing like a roof," Grandmother answered.

"Well, Mother Pérez, you could take the money from us or get a home improvement loan," Mom suggested.

Grandfather's face darkened. "There were no debts on this house when I inherited it from my father. There will be none when my son inherits it. I want no more talk of loans."

"I'm sorry," my mother murmured. "Juan and I just wanted to help."

Grandfather nodded, but his proud expression didn't change.

Then Grandmother served chicken with olive sauce flavored with oregano and coriander. For dessert she gave us *leche quemada*. While eating the milk and almond pudding, Dad and Grandfather started arguing about the Big Little Books.

"I haven't thought about those things for years, Father. Why, they'd have been thrown away if *Mamacita* hadn't packed them in a box and lugged them up to the attic," Dad told him.

"No matter, Juan, they are yours. I remember you bought some of them with your paper route money," Grandfather said stiffly.

"Then charge me storage," Dad replied. "That'll add up to more money than you'll get for them."

"Now, Juan. Now, Father Pérez," Mom interrupted in a soft, lilting voice. "Let's not spoil this good dinner by arguing."

"All right, *acushla*," Dad answered, smiling at my mother. "As for those Big Little Books, I'd forgotten I ever had them."

Grandfather's back was stiff as a broomstick. "It's not just that," he said. "There are the Olssens who are coming tomorrow. Nancy says they'll help us with the sale, but I think we should pay them. Besides that, I don't want Luisa to sell her possessions."

Grandmother's eyes snapped as she looked at him. "For years you've been telling me that the attic was cluttered with junk. Maybe it's not junk, but we don't need most of it. I rather like the idea of people who will use and enjoy them having Great-aunt Maria's linens and vases. Goodness knows, I've tried for years to get Juan's wife here to take some of the stuff stored up there."

Mom reached over and patted Grandmother's hand. "I appreciate your offer, but I just don't have any desire to own antiques. Too much dusting. Too much clutter, and too much care."

Grandmother glanced over at her china cabinet and so did I. "That's one task I must get at," she said. "It *is* a mess! So jammed with vases, figurines, dishes, and crystal that no one can see how pretty some of them are. I just keep putting more in it. Gifts, raffle prizes. I don't even know where it all comes from."

I was staring at the bottom shelf. There, in the back, sat a vase. A dull, soft rose, it resembled one Mrs. Olssen had shown me. I slid from my chair and went to the cabinet, giving Grandmother a glance that asked permission to open it.

She nodded, and I lifted out the vase, careful not to touch the hand-painted cups and saucers that stood in front of it. The glaze felt right—a soft glaze that almost melted into my hand. Holding my breath, I turned it over, then whistled when I saw the reversed RP and the flame marks. "I suspected it might be Rookwood," I said, handing it to Grandmother. "Mrs. Olssen collects Rookwood, but she doesn't have one like this. Where did you get it?"

Grandmother shook her head. "I can't remember. I've had it for years."

"What is Rookwood, anyway?" Mom asked as Grandmother handed her the vase.

"It's an art pottery that was made by the Rookwood Pottery Company in Cincinnati," I said slowly, trying to remember just what Mrs. Olssen had told me. "The company was started in 1880 by a Mrs. Storer. Some of the vases are quite valuable. Mrs. Olssen said many people collect it."

"You said Mrs. Olssen collects it?" Grandfather asked.

I nodded.

"Do you want to keep the vase, Luisa?" He turned to my grandmother.

"I can't even remember where it came from. I'd planned to donate it to a rummage sale."

I shuddered and reached for the vase.

"I seem to recall its being in my mother's house," she continued. "No, I don't want to keep it. I don't even like the color."

I looked at the bottom again. "According to what Mrs. Olssen told me, the markings mean this one was made in 1902."

Grandfather looked thoughtful. "If the Olssens will help us price, and Nancy doesn't think they'd take money, perhaps Mrs. Olssen would like to have the vase."

Grandmother nodded, with a smile.

Dad seemed pleased and amused. "So there are other people with a lot of stiff-necked pride around," he said. "Well, Father, right now I'm donating the box of books to Nancy and Tomás. You can argue with them about it."

Tomás and I exchanged troubled glances. We already had enough to worry about with Grandmother insisting that all the money from our own belongings had to go to us without Dad adding the Big Little Books to our problems. I'll have to admit that the thought of buying the silver bracelet, if Mr. Jackson would make another one, crossed my mind again, but then I remembered the roof. It was more important to help pay for a new roof.

꽃꽃꽃 **14** 꽃꽃꽃

I raced straight from school to Grandmother's house the next day, hoping that the boys would hurry. Grandmother had asked Tomás to bring Pete.

I was worried about the meeting between the two ladies. Grandfather, I felt, would find Mr. Olssen a kindred soul because they were both interested in tools and handicrafts. I feared that some sort of resentment was building on Grandmother's part. If only Tomás would keep quiet about Mrs. Olssen's melt-in-your-mouth Swedish cookies!

When I went through the dining room, I realized that I was right. Grandmother had gone overboard! The table was spread with her best lace cloth and set with a dessert service. There was a silver tray heaped with *empanadas* stuffed with cream cheese and chicken and a plate covered with *churros*. In the middle of the table sat a flan circled with frosted grapes and, next to it, a coconut cake. In the kitchen, Grandmother was fixing both hot chocolate and coffee. I threw my free arm around her. "You've really outdone yourself," I said. "I'm glad I didn't have much lunch."

"Why didn't you eat?" she asked sharply. "You're just skin and bone now."

I laughed. Grandmother always said that when I refused a second helping. "I'm dumpy and five pounds overweight," I said, hating to admit it, but knowing that it was true.

"That's just baby fat," she said, contradicting herself. "You have lovely features."

"You're prejudiced," I answered with another one-handed hug. "The table looks lovely. Can I help?"

Grandmother took off her apron. "You can watch for the Olssens while I get your grandfather out of the basement. Men and their tools. He has put back half of what he was going to sell."

The Olssens were coming up the walk when I reached the front window. I called to Grandmother who hurried into the living room. I sort of stammered out the introductions, wishing that Tomás were there to help me. I'm never good at that sort of thing, and always think of what I should have said several hours later.

"I've wondered who lived in this lovely house,"

Mrs. Olssen said with a wide smile. "Olaf and I have admired it ever since we moved to Santo Rosario."

Just then Tomás and Pete bounced up the steps and Grandfather entered the room. After a general flurry of greetings, Tomás told Grandmother he was hungry.

"Everything is ready in the dining room," Grandmother said, motioning us through the door. Mrs. Olssen's eyes widened a bit when she saw the table, and I kept hoping the visit would go all right.

"A flan! Wow, *Abuelita*, you always know when the food at school has been bad," Tomás said. "I'm starving."

"So am I," Pete added. "You're the world's best cook, Mrs. Pérez."

"That school!" Grandmother answered. "I cannot see why the food should be so bad." She turned to Mrs. Olssen. "Tomás raves about your cookies. The ones he calls *spritz bak—spritz* something or other."

"*Spritz baklese,*" Mrs. Olssen murmured in a soft voice. She pointed to the silver tray. "Are those *empan —empond*—I don't know how to pronounce it, but Pete and Tomás claim no one in the world can make them the way you do. I have been longing to taste one."

"You must have more than one." Grandmother's tone was much warmer.

Mr. Olssen had already sampled one. "Could you give Iris the recipe, Mrs. Pérez? Now I know why Tomás talks so much about your cooking."

Grandmother unbent all the way. "I'll teach you to make them some day soon," she said to Mrs. Olssen. "You must come over and spend a morning with me."

I grinned at Tomás and relaxed. Mr. Olssen and Grandfather were busy talking about leatherwork and wood carving. They soon left the table and headed for the basement to go over the tools. Tomás and Pete finished off the last of the flan while Mrs. Olssen and Grandmother drank second cups of coffee. Then Tomás and Pete clattered down the basement steps and we climbed to the attic.

"I really think I should call the Goodwill," Grandmother said as she opened the door. "I've been sorting things, and I've found four trunks filled with old clothes."

"Don't call anyone until we have a chance to look over all of it," Mrs. Olssen advised. "What kind of old clothes are they?"

"Some of my mother's, some that I think were my grandmother's, and some that belonged to Great-aunt Maria Sanchez." She turned to me. "You and Jean used to play dress-up in them."

I shook my head. "No. We played with *your* old clothes and some of your hats. You wouldn't let us into the trunks that had your mother's dresses in them."

Grandmother looked uncertain for a moment. "I wonder why I was saving them. You and Jean always looked so cute when you came downstairs wearing those big hats. How is Jean feeling now?"

"She's home. I talked to her on the phone last night and she says she feels fine. Her mother won't let me visit her because the doctor ordered rest for several more days."

"I'm glad she's better. Now then, Mrs. Olssen, Nancy says some of these old things are valuable. I've put out a lot of china and glassware on that table." She pointed toward a golden oak dining table that I knew had come from Great-aunt Maria's house. Its matching sideboard stood behind it.

Mrs. Olssen picked up the tea-leaf compote. "You should get at least seventy-five dollars for this," she said. "Of course that isn't its full value, but you can't hope to get that. Are you certain that you want to sell these lovely pieces?"

Grandmother nodded, her mouth set in determined lines. "We must have a new roof before the rains come. The estimate was over eleven hundred dollars. We have only one hundred seventy in the roof fund."

I did some quick mental arithmetic and my heart sort of thudded to my ankles. Almost a thousand dollars. I think I moaned because Mrs. Olssen gave me a funny look.

"Are there chairs to match this table?" she asked briskly.

"Behind those trunks and barrels. Six of them," Grandmother said.

Mrs. Olssen smiled. "Then I think you are a long way toward your goal. You should get close to five hundred dollars for this set, if you want to sell it."

Grandmother gasped. I saw a tear roll down her cheek as she turned away and flung open a trunk. "Here are some clothes, Mrs. Olssen. Some of them date back to 1922 when I was married." She unrolled a bundle of blue tissue and laid a white dress over the lid of the trunk and then picked up a mantilla made of fragile creamy lace. "This I wore for my wedding."

"Surely you don't want to sell that," Mrs. Olssen said softly.

"No. I'm hoping to see Nancy wear it one day." She draped the mantilla over my head. "There's a tortoise comb in my jewelry box that goes with it."

"It's very beautiful, *Abuelita*," I said, "but I won't need it for years and years. I'm going to be an engineer before I marry."

Mrs. Olssen's laugh pealed through the attic. "You'll fall in love and forget about all that."

I shook my head. "Oh, I'll fall in love, I suppose, but

that's not going to change my mind. I'm going to be an engineer and work on rocket ships and, maybe some day, go into space."

"These girls! In my day we all wanted to be nurses or teachers." Grandmother folded the mantilla, then ruffled my hair. "Such big dreams, *chiquita mía*, but you've always been good with figures. Maybe we'll let you handle the money the day of the sale."

"That's what we'd better do right now," Mrs. Olssen suggested, looking into the trunk. "Get back to planning the sale. There's such a craze for nostalgia, with people collecting clothes from the twenties and thirties, that some of these dresses will bring a good price." She went back to the oak table and started looking over the dishes, vases, and glassware. "Depression glass, cut glass, pattern glass," she murmured. "And lots of lovely old china. I think Olaf and I had better spend several days over here pricing these things and maybe sorting out some that you should keep."

"We must not take up too much of your time," Grandmother said.

"Don't worry about that. I don't have enough to do to take up my time. Besides, you promised to teach me how to make *empanadas,*" she added, pronouncing the word carefully.

I was thirsty so I left the two ladies in the attic and

went downstairs, hoping that there'd be some hot chocolate left. Tomás and Pete were sitting at the kitchen table, each polishing off a huge piece of coconut cake. "How can you two possibly swallow another bite?" I asked.

Pete grinned at me. "Who could resist your grandmother's cake?"

I discovered that they'd finished the hot chocolate, too, so I poured myself a glass of milk.

"Tomás, give us a hand down here, please," Grandfather called through the half-opened door to the basement.

"Be right there." Tomás crammed a forkful of cake into his mouth and ran downstairs.

I slid onto the chair opposite Pete. "Things appear to be going well. Grandmother seems to be warming up to Mrs. Olssen."

He nodded. "Nancy, this garage sale bit started me thinking about having one of my own to help come up with the car insurance money. I filled a couple of cartons with books, games, and some old sweaters. But there's not enough to pay to advertise it, so I thought I'd donate it to your grandparents' sale."

I straightened in my chair. "You will not!"

"Why not? I spend a lot of time here, and I think your grandparents are great."

"Grandmother would not allow it, and neither would I."

"Oh, come on, Nancy. I'm just trying to help." Pete kept his voice down, but I could see that he was getting angry. "Your grandparents wouldn't need to know. We'll just lump my junk in with yours."

"That won't work, either. Grandmother has already refused to accept any money we make from our things. The grandparents are proud people."

"Seems to me they aren't the only ones," Pete snapped. "That neck of yours is pretty stiff right now."

I grinned at him. "Just about as stiff as my cast."

Pete smiled back. "Okay. Maybe I can hitch a ride to the flea market with the Olssens and sell my stuff there. One thing you can't do. You can't stop me from helping with the garage sale."

I didn't want to fight with Pete. "You know we want you. We've already asked you to help."

𝕏 **15** 𝕏

The morning of the garage sale came almost before I knew it. I stretched lazily when the alarm went off, then jumped out of bed. I bumped my cast against the closet door and muttered angrily. I wished again that Jim Block had wound up wearing the lump of plaster that I was stuck with for another few weeks.

I pulled on jeans and blouse, thinking that I was getting pretty good at this one-handed business, picked up my shoes, and hurried to the kitchen. Maybe some people can tie shoelaces with one hand, but I hadn't mastered it yet. Tomás was there ahead of me, drinking a glass of milk. "We'd better hurry," he said.

"The ad in the paper said nine o'clock, and I want some breakfast," I answered, opening the refrigerator.

"The ad also said antiques, and Mr. Olssen told us

people may come early. We had better get going right now."

Sometimes there's just no arguing with Tomás. I grabbed an apple and flung my jacket over my shoulders. We'd planned to walk the mile to our grandparents' house, but just then Dad entered the kitchen. "I'll give you a lift," he offered.

Tomás tied my shoelaces and told me he was getting tired of playing lady's maid.

"Not as tired as I am of this cast," I said and went out to the car.

As we drove down the street, I had a terrible thought. "What if no one comes?" I asked.

"I wouldn't worry about that," Dad answered. "From what I hear about garage sales, your big worry may be how to handle the crowd."

"The Olssens have everything figured out," Tomás explained. "They laid out the garage like a store."

"I'm in charge of the cashbox," I announced proudly. "We have twenty dollars worth of change to start with."

"What did you decide to do about the Big Little Books?" Dad asked.

"We didn't win that battle," Tomás answered. "Grandfather wouldn't agree to lumping our cast-offs in with theirs. Mrs. Olssen worked out a system. My things are tagged with an x before the price, and Nan's with a y. Jean is going to help Nan with the money, and she'll keep track of the x and y tags."

When we reached our grandparents' house, Dad parked across the street. "It'll be half an hour before your mother is ready to leave, so I'll stick around. Maybe I can help," he said.

The Olssens were already there. Mrs. Olssen was setting up a card table just outside the garage door and Mr. Olssen came out carrying two folding chairs. I knew that would be my post. I told Dad that the card table was the cashier's office and introduced him to the Olssens.

When he asked if he could do anything to help, Mrs. Olssen told Dad to put up our signs, one in front of the house and the others at the nearest corners. Tomás helped Grandfather and Mr. Olssen place the oak dining-room set on the lawn at the edge of the driveway.

Jean arrived at eight-thirty. "It seems like forever since I've seen you," I said, giving her a big hug. "I stopped at your house after school Thursday, but your mother wouldn't let me in. She said you were napping. How are you?"

"I'm fine," Jean answered. "The only thing is that I have this horror of getting into a car."

I nodded. I knew exactly how she felt.

Grandmother came out the back door and hurried over to Jean. She hugged her, patted her hair, then insisted that Jean sit right down and rest. Finally I asked Grandmother if she had made any hot chocolate.

"Didn't you eat breakfast?" she questioned, her tone indicating that I had committed a major crime.

"Tomás dragged me off before I had a chance," I admitted.

She went back into the house and I looked at Jean with a broad smile. "Wow, I've missed you! Be sure to tell me if you feel tired. Grandmother will find a place for you to lie down."

"You sound just like my mother. She wasn't going to let me come. Luckily I had an appointment with the doctor yesterday. He said I was all right and told Mother to stop coddling me. How is your arm?"

"A nuisance, but it doesn't hurt."

Jean looked at the furniture on the lawn, then bent forward so she could see into the garage. "It's just like a store," she said. "And there's so much stuff. How did you ever get it priced and set up so fast?"

"The Olssens helped all week and we worked on it after school." I leaned back in the chair, remembering the many trips Tomás and Pete had made to bring down Grandmother's treasures from the attic, while I sat at the dining room table writing out price tags for piles and piles of linens. There had been old pictures —among them a girl with a robin and one that Mrs. Olssen excitedly called a Maxfield Parrish print.

She had told my grandparents that some of the small tables and night stands tucked away in the corners of the attic were gems. She insisted that Grandmother keep Great-aunt Maria's marble-topped table and sell instead a nondescript end table from the living room.

The Olssens had brought over card tables and the grandparents borrowed more from my parents. Fortunately Grandfather had enlarged the original garage years ago, so it was large enough for us to display the wares from the attic, plus the duplicate tools he had decided to sell. Mrs. Olssen even suggested selling some of the old trunks. She said that the dome-topped ones were collector's items.

Grandmother had washed stacks of dusty glassware and china from the barrels. Mrs. Olssen urged her to keep some glassware, especially the pieces she called Diamond Point, but Grandmother shook her head and told her the roof was more important. I smiled at the memory of the two ladies, who were becoming fast friends, arguing gently over what to keep and what to sell.

Jean stood up and went into the garage. "Those vases and cups are pretty, but my, the prices are high," she said when she returned.

"I know. They seemed mighty steep to me, too, but Mrs. Olssen explained that she put higher than usual garage sale prices on the best pieces because a dealer or collector might stop by. She said Grandmother should get, at the least, close to what a dealer would pay. The Olssens are neat people, and they really know about antiques."

Jean nodded. She leaned close to me. "Tell me what else you've been doing. When are we going to get back into the detecting business?"

I laughed. "Weren't the flea market and the accident enough for you?"

Her eyebrows almost touched as she frowned. "I've had plenty of time to think about what happened, and I'm completely certain that Jim Block is mixed up with those people you saw. He was responsible for landing me in the hospital, and I'm determined to get back at him for it."

Jean's usually smiling face had a deep frown on it. I was surprised because I had never known her to be vindictive. Then I remembered that Marylyn Stone had taken over her part in the class play. I patted her hand. "There'll be many more plays with good parts for you," I said.

She sort of choked. "I heard Marylyn was great, too."

Pete wheeled in on his ten-speed as Grandmother brought out a tray with hot chocolate and rolls on it. "I see I arrived at exactly the right time," he said.

I grinned at him. "You and Tomás have stomachs

like quicksand—bottomless."

"You had better finish that hot chocolate in a hurry," he answered as four cars pulled up in front of the house. "Customers."

Jean and I drained our cups, and she carried the tray back to the kitchen while I watched the bargain hunters disappear into the garage. My mouth went dry and I hoped I wouldn't goof making change. Before Jean came back, the first customer had given me three dollars for two of Grandmother's hand-painted cups and saucers. Suddenly the place was filled with people and Jean was writing down the prices from the x and y tags while I added up purchases and made change as fast as I could, thinking that if this kept up I could use an adding machine. In a short while it thinned out, and Mrs. Olssen walked over to us. "The next bunch of customers will be here soon," she said. "You'll find it goes in spurts. Is everything all right?"

I nodded, glad of the slack period. Then a second batch of cars drove up and the garage and yard were filled with people again. I saw my pet hate, the whispering woman, go by and heard her say to her companion that she hoped there was something good here. I nudged Jean. "Remember her?"

Jean grimaced. "At least she won't get all kinds of treasures for nothing here."

Then we were too busy to talk. We sold tools, picture frames, a velvet jacket trimmed with an ornamental braid that Mrs. Olssen called soutache, and the hats that Jean and I had played with. One man bought ten of the Big Little Books for fifty dollars. I started thinking about the hammered silver bracelet. Just then the whispering woman came up with a box filled with china. I could see the tea-leaf compote in one corner. "I'll give you thirty-five dollars for this lot," she said, pulling the money out of her purse.

"I can't take any offers," I protested. "Everything is priced."

"Nonsense," she snapped. "Everyone takes offers at garage sales." She dropped the money on the table and picked up the box.

I jumped up, knocking over my chair. "Mrs. Olssen! Pete!" I called. "Please come here."

Jean moved around the table to block the woman. Mrs. Olssen came running from the back-porch steps, and Pete raced out of the garage.

"What's all this?" Mrs. Olssen asked.

I started to explain and the whispering woman interrupted in a voice that could be heard two blocks away. "Get out of my way!" she shouted. "I paid for these items."

"She didn't. She offered thirty-five dollars, and I told her no. The tea-leaf compote is in that box, and it is marked more than that, and I don't even know what else she has there." I was getting teary as I explained. Everyone was looking at me.

Suddenly Grandfather was there. He removed the box from the woman's arms and set it on the table.

Mrs. Olssen picked up the thirty-five dollars and handed it to her. "You can buy the merchandise at the prices marked or you can leave right now," she said.

"The prices are too high. I made a fair offer," the woman insisted.

"We'll see." Mrs. Olssen took the tea-leaf compote from the box. "That's seventy-five dollars. This RS Prussia plate is twenty-five. That's a hundred. This pair of figurines makes it a hundred twenty-five." She continued in a voice that was icy cold, "I've seen you operate before. You'd go straight from here to the Early Times Shoppe and sell these things at a profit. Now, it's either pay us one hundred twenty-five dollars or leave."

The woman's face was bright red. She spun around as if to go, then turned back, opened her purse, and took out her billfold. She slapped the money down in front of me, grabbed up the box, and stalked down the driveway.

"Whew!" I said. "I hope we don't have any more customers like that one."

Mrs. Olssen patted my shoulder. "You two handled it just fine."

Pete picked up my chair. "Good work, Nancy."

I started to get that puffed head feeling, then remembered that I hadn't done anything except call for help. I sat down and made change for a lady who was buying three of my outgrown dresses for fifty cents each.

Noon arrived almost before I knew it. Mrs. Olssen walked up to us with a paper bag in her hand. "Your grandmother has lunch ready so I'll relieve you two while you eat. But first let's take out all the paper money except enough to change a twenty. You can go into the kitchen and count it." She scooped the bills into the bag for me. "We'll count the change later."

Jean and I hurried into the kitchen. I sniffed the aroma of *sopa de albóndigas* and smiled. It had been a chilly morning and meatball soup would taste good.

Grandfather was sitting at the kitchen table, a bowl of steaming soup in front of him. "How are we doing?" he asked.

I held up the bag. "Want to help us count?"

"No, I'll leave it to you and Jean. Why don't you use the dining-room table?"

"We know there's a hundred twenty-five dollars," I said to Jean as I dumped out the bills.

"There's a lot more than that," she said. "Let's make piles of a hundred dollars each."

I agreed and started separating the bills into ones,

fives, tens, and twenties while Jean watched. Then I counted a hundred dollars in twenties and asked her to recheck. When we finished we had six piles and seventy-one dollars extra. "That's not enough," I whispered. "I thought we had more than that."

"It's only noon," Jean said. "More people will come."

Grandmother had our soup on the table when we went back to the kitchen. "How much have we made?" she asked.

"Six hundred seventy-one dollars," I answered. "And there's a lot of change in the cashbox to count yet."

Her shoulders drooped. "I hoped we had made more money than that."

"It's early yet. Besides, no one has bought the oak dining-room set. Once we sell that, we'll have more than enough for the roof." I sat down, picked up my spoon, and blew on the soup.

"What if no one buys it?" she asked, worry lines creasing her forehead.

"Mrs. Olssen said someone would, and she's been right so far." I started eating my soup, wishing she'd stop worrying.

Grandfather put his napkin on the table. "I'll relieve Mr. Olssen so he can eat."

Just then Tomás and Pete came in for lunch. "Wow,

that turkey roasting in your oven smells good, Mrs. Pérez," Pete said. "I can hardly wait for dinner."

How she had found time I didn't know, but Grandmother did have a turkey roasting. She had invited the Olssens, my family, Jean, and Pete for dinner. To celebrate, she'd said. I hoped that it would really be a celebration, that we would have all of the money we needed for the roof fund.

By four-thirty it didn't seem that we would be celebrating. A good many people had stopped by during the afternoon, but the cash customers had bought small items. Several couples had looked at the oak dining-room furniture, and one young man offered two hundred dollars for it.

At Mrs. Olssen's insistence, Grandmother had refused the offer, but she looked doubtful.

"I know you can get three hundred fifty from a secondhand dealer. It's worth more, and there's no point in taking any less than that," Mrs. Olssen told her.

I left my table and walked to the garage door. About a third of the china, knick-knacks, clothes, and vases were still there and half of the Big Little Books. I turned back to Jean, who was adding a long column of figures. She smiled at me. "The x tags add up to ninety-four dollars," she announced.

"Wow! What's Tomás' total?"

"I'll have it in a minute." She added the y column, then looked at me. "You beat him. The y tags only come to fifty-one dollars."

"Next time Mom calls me a pack rat, I'll remind her that my miserly habit made me ninety-four dollars. Then there's half of the fifty from the Big Little Books so I have a total of one hundred nineteen dollars!"

"What are you going to do with all that money?"

"First thing after school Monday I'm going to the Senior Citizens Co-op and see if Mr. Jackson will make another silver bracelet like the one I told you about." Then I looked into the cashbox doubtfully. It didn't seem to me that we had taken in another six hundred dollars. What would we do if we didn't have enough money for the roof?

At five o'clock the sale was over. Pete and Tomás helped Grandfather and Mr. Olssen carry the oak furniture into the garage. Jean followed me into the house and I put the cashbox down on the kitchen table.

Mrs. Olssen and Grandmother set the dining-room table while Jean and I counted the money. We had three hundred dollars and seventy-five cents in the cashbox.

Tomás and Pete sat down opposite us just as we finished. "How much does it come to?" Tomás asked.

"Nine hundred and seventy-one dollars," I whispered. "That includes our money."

Tomás lowered his voice. "Is there enough altogether to pay for the roof?"

I shut all thought of the bracelet out of my mind. "Grandmother said she had saved a hundred seventy dollars. Yes, the total is enough."

Tomás leaned closer. "We'll forget about those x and y tags. All of the money goes to the grandparents."

I nodded.

Grandmother came into the kitchen, opened the oven door, and basted the turkey. "It'll be just right at six o'clock," she said, coming over to the table. "What's the grand total?"

Tomás grabbed her around the waist and swung her in a circle. Then he set her down in a chair and put the cashbox in her lap. "You can call the roofer tomorrow. There's over nine hundred dollars here."

Grandmother's eyes glistened. "I must tell your grandfather. He has been so worried." Her smile was bright as she turned to me. "How much money did you make, Nancy?"

"Why, ah . . . "

Tomás interrupted my stammered attempt at evasion. "We didn't sell much of our stuff," he said. "Not enough to count so we just lumped it in with yours."

Grandmother looked at Tomás with grave eyes.

"You sold a lot of Big Little Books. I saw a man give Nancy fifty dollars for some of them."

"We sold only a few games, *Abuelita*, and there's almost half a box of Big Little Books left," Tomás evaded.

"Nancy, exactly how much of this money is yours?" Grandmother's voice permitted nothing but a truthful answer.

"One hundred nineteen dollars," I said in a small voice.

"How much belongs to Tomás?"

"Seventy-six dollars."

Grandmother was silent for a moment. "Then we are short about two hundred dollars of the roof money." With great dignity she stood up and walked over to the stove. She checked the turkey, then turned on the burner under the potatoes.

Tomás went over to her. "But *Abuelita* . . . "

"We will not discuss it, Tomás. We told you in the beginning that we did not take money for selling things that do not belong to us."

I heard the front door open and realized that Dad and Mom must be coming in. I shoved my chair back and raced through the dining room. Maybe they could talk some sense into Grandmother.

🎭🎭 16 🎭🎭

Dad shrugged his shoulders when I explained the problem.

Mom patted my cheek. "We'll have to think of something. Right now let's be cheerful and enjoy your grandmother's good food." She disappeared through the kitchen door.

"Guess I'll find Father and Mr. Olssen," Dad said. "Maybe they need some help."

Tomás, Jean, Pete, and I stared at one another. "Come on. Think. There must be something we can do," Pete said.

Jean twirled a lock of her long hair around her fingers. "I've always loved that attic. We can't let it get all wet with rain. Maybe we could have another garage sale."

"That wouldn't work, not right away," I said, looking down at the floor. "Mrs. Olssen told me that generally the same group of people go to garage sales. In a small town like this we wouldn't have enough new customers to make a repeat sale worthwhile. Besides, there's the expense of advertising it and the work of setting it up again. Grandfather said he wanted to get everything left packed in boxes tomorrow so he could return all of the tables he borrowed."

Jean's lips turned down at the corners and Pete scratched his head. "If only that robbery hadn't happened," he said.

"How much were the stolen things worth?" Tomás asked me.

"I don't know for certain. Over a couple of hundred dollars worth of the merchandise belonged to the grandparents, I guess. Why?"

"We must get back to detecting. If we could recover the afghans, sweaters, and leather purses and belts, Grandmother could take them back to the Co-op and sell them. Then they would have all of the money they need. We must track down this Buck Seymour. He's our only lead," Tomás said, his eyes flashing.

"I won't be much good at detecting until I get this bothersome cast off my arm," I said bitterly. "Last time we tried I got bumped all over the place by that Jim Block. Remember?"

"What did he do to you?" Pete's voice sounded angry.

Tomás related the incident and then returned to the subject at hand. "I have a list of eight Seymour and one Seymore addresses. We must check out each one and try to tie that blue-and-white station wagon or Buck Seymour to one of the addresses."

"That won't prove they are the thieves," I objected. "What do we do then?"

"Then we make like Apaches and creep in during the silence of the night and search," Tomás said.

"There's no chance of that," I said. "You know we aren't allowed out at night alone."

"People aren't always at home. We could watch the place during the day and then look in the windows when they leave," Pete suggested.

"At least that wouldn't be breaking and entering," I said.

Jean shook her head so violently her long blonde hair flew over her face. "If all four of us start hanging around one block or one corner, the first thing that will happen is that someone will call the police. People are scared these days."

"No one pays any attention to a boy and girl walking down the street holding hands," Pete said thoughtfully. "If the girl leans against a tree and has a long conversation with the boy, people just walk by with a smile on their faces."

"You mean stage a romantic scene?" Jean giggled, looking at my brother.

Tomás sort of glared at her. "What are you suggesting—that I put on a fake act with you?"

Jean sighed and leaned over toward him, gazing into his eyes. "Come on now, Tomás," she said in her best ingenue voice. "You can pretend, can't you? Especially when it's to help your grandparents?"

"Sure, Tomás," Pete said. "You've been giving us all this talk about the greatness of Latins. You can pretend to be a great Latin lover."

Tomás looked at Jean again, almost as if seeing her for the first time. "It might be fun at that."

"Stop shilly-shallying, Tomás," I snapped. "If I can walk around staring moon-eyed at Pete, you can do the same with Jean. What we need is a cover, and Pete came up with a good one."

Mom came back into the room with a cup of coffee in her hand. "There's still hope," she told us. "Your grandparents are going to the flea market next week end with the Olssens. They'll take several boxes of things to sell."

"But it might rain before next week end," I wailed. "If only they weren't so stubborn."

Mom's face was pensive. "You and Tomás can't just give them the money. But maybe, if you approached them privately, in a business-like manner, about a loan . . . ?" Her voice trailed off on a questioning note.

I smiled at Tomás and he nodded. "I'll talk to Grandfather man to man."

🙈🙈 **17** 🙈🙈

Jean and Pete arrived at our house about two o'clock the next afternoon. Tomás had our assignments ready. He gave Pete and me the closest Seymour addresses. He and Jean took the ones farthest away because they could use their bikes.

"You're going to be mighty conspicuous swooping around on your ten-speeds," I warned.

"We're not that dumb," Tomás said. "We can walk the bikes and be deep in conversation."

Pete held the door open. "Let them worry about it. Let's get started."

I picked up my jacket and went down the steps, wishing that I didn't have the cast on my arm. I had put on my best brown pants, but I couldn't wear the matching top because of the narrow sleeve. I had brushed my hair smooth and had even scrubbed my teeth extra hard, wondering if the television commercials were right. Then I'd laughed at myself. This wasn't a *date*. We were on detective duty and Pete was the same Pete Higgins I had known all my life. Then I wondered why he had become so angry when he heard that Jim had rammed my bumper car.

We walked toward the first Seymour address in silence. My tongue felt like a lump of lead and my throat was dry. Come off it, I said to myself. This isn't a boy. This is Pete, your friend.

"I think it's in the next block. It's 821 State Street, isn't it?" Pete asked.

"Yes. What are we going to talk about while we do this scene?" I was wishing that Jean had written some lines for us.

"We'll think of something. Football scores or the weather. Say, did you manage to change your grandparents' minds about the money?"

We were about three houses away from the address. Pete took my hand and steered me across the street. I leaned against a tree and smiled up at him. He put his hand on the tree just above my shoulder. "Now that should convince anyone," he said, looking at the house. "You didn't answer my question."

"Tomás handled that. He made out a short term note with six per cent interest. Said he'd learned about it in Business Math. Grandfather signed it, and they'll call the roofer tomorrow." I looked up at the sky. It was bright blue with a veiling of low, scuddy clouds. "We've been fortunate about the weather," I added.

"Good, that's one problem solved," he said, smiling down at me. "Now, if we're lucky, we'll spot that blue-and-white station wagon of yours."

"Not mine," I protested. "In fact, I would just as soon not spot that Buck Seymour again, either. He gives me the crawlies." I was beginning to feel shivers in my toes, and I wondered why I had ever wanted to play detective.

"There doesn't seem to be any sign of life in that house," Pete said. "Let's walk to the corner slowly, then come back on the other side of the street. Maybe we can see into the garage."

We passed a man weeding a flower bed. Pete gave him a smile and an easy hello. My throat was dried up again and I felt my face getting warm when Pete rattled off something about a picnic next Saturday.

"It's past the picnic season," I objected.

"The four of us can have a fire and hot dogs at the beach," he said. "You bring the hot dogs, and I'll build the fire."

We had reached the corner by that time and were out of earshot of the weeding man. "See how easy it is," Pete said. "No one pays attention."

"You mean that picnic talk was all window dressing?"

"Sure was, but it's not a bad idea."

"Well, I'll build the fire; you bring the hot dogs," I snapped.

"Hey, don't get mad. You're supposed to have a romantic interest in me. Remember that cover we talked about. We're detecting." Pete's grin was infuriating.

"Yes, and at this rate we'll be detecting next week, too." I was annoyed with myself for taking him seriously. We both looked at the house. The garage door was closed. The front window shades were pulled halfway down.

"I just don't think this is it," I said. "It's too neat. It doesn't look like a place where Buck Seymour would live."

"I don't think anyone's home," Pete said. "Let's try the next address."

I agreed and we went down the street, turned the corner, and hiked ten blocks to High Street. The neighborhood here was deteriorating. The houses needed paint and the shrubbery was overgrown, the flower beds neglected.

"This looks promising," Pete said. He took my hand again, and I smiled up at him, wishing that Jean could observe my great acting. Suddenly Pete gave a long, low whistle. "I think we're getting warm. Isn't that Jim Block getting out of that car across the street?"

"It sure is. What is he doing driving? He lost his license, didn't he?"

"I thought he did." Pete tightened his grip on my hand. "He's seen us. Now we really put on an act. Pretend you haven't seen him."

We walked on a few steps, and Pete started talking about a television show he had watched last night. I checked the house numbers and saw that the address we wanted was two houses away. Then Jim was beside us.

"What are you two up to?" he asked. "And what is baby sister doing out without her brother for a protector?"

"What are *you* up to?" Pete shot back.

"Had to deliver a message from my father to one of his clients who doesn't have a telephone. You know, do the old man a favor," Jim explained. "I've got the car for the rest of the day so I'll give you a lift wherever you want to go."

"My parents have issued a strict edict about getting into your car." I looked straight at Jim and chopped off each word.

His face reddened. "You don't have to get mean about it."

"It's a nice afternoon to walk and talk." Pete's manner was easy. "So long, Jim."

We continued down the block, past the large house which looked, from the mailboxes on the porch, to be cut into four apartments. "We could check the names on the boxes," I suggested.

"No. Jim's sitting in his car watching us. Let's go back to your house and hold a conference with Tomás and Jean."

"You mean you think this is the right place?"

"It must be. What would Jim be doing here if he hadn't come to meet that scrawny-faced guy you described? I don't believe that bit about a message. He had just driven up when he saw us," Pete said.

"But that doesn't mean anything. It's not proof of anything," I argued. "We haven't seen the blue-and-white station wagon."

By now we had reached the corner. Pete still held my hand. "Let's go down the street behind the house," he suggested. "We may see something from there."

We walked to the end of the block and turned into the next street. "It was the third house," Pete said.

"This won't do any good." I pointed to a high fence.

"Even if we haven't found the car, this must be the right place."

"Oh, we're dumb," I said. "Of course we wouldn't see the car. It's the middle of Sunday afternoon. They are probably at the Los Olivos flea market selling all that stolen goods."

"Then what would Jim be doing here? I'll bet that station wagon is parked in back of the house."

"Shall we go all the way around the block and try to get another look?"

"Not with Jim hanging around. He's suspicious enough already," Pete said.

A car turned the corner and slowed up beside us. I shivered as I saw Jim grinning at us. "Changed your mind about that ride yet?" he called.

"Three's a crowd," Pete answered. "Nancy and I have some serious talking to do about going together."

Jim waved a hand and drove slowly down the street. I looked at Pete, stunned. "Why did you say a thing like that? It'll be all over your school tomorrow and mine the next day."

"Had to give him something to think about. Now act as if you were my girl. He's coming around the block again."

We walked slowly toward my house, and I clung to Pete's hand. I wasn't really acting. I was scared. Jim Block went past us four times, and his car was sitting across the street when we reached my door.

Tomás and Jean were in the family room listening to records. "It took you long enough," Tomás said.

"We didn't have wheels, remember, but we did get

results." I was still jumpy and my voice was sharp.

Tomás turned down the record player. "You really found them? You saw the car?"

"No, but we're almost certain of the address. It's the one on High Street," Pete said and went on to explain about seeing Jim Block and how he had followed us home.

"You mean he's actually sitting out there in front now?" Tomás asked.

"He was when we came inside," I said.

Jean looked scared. "Why would he be watching us?"

I giggled. "What a fine bunch of detectives we are. We start out trying to detect and now we're being detected."

"It's not funny," Jean said with a quaver in her voice. "Jim Block reminds me of something that has crawled out of a swamp. I would just as soon never see him."

"You know, Tomás, there is something odd about the guy," Pete said thoughtfully. "He has absolutely no friends. You're about the only one at school who talks to him."

"He's having a bad time getting adjusted, and I think he has parent problems," Tomás explained. "No one gives him a chance. I don't think it's fair of you three to jump to conclusions."

"He does too have friends," I interrupted. "What about Buck Seymour and that girl with the braids? I'm sure he was warning them at the flea market, and what about his actions today? I'd call them suspicious."

Tomás appeared doubtful. "I don't know. Maybe he was lonely and wanted company."

"All this is getting us no place," I said. "What are we going to do now?"

Jean looked down at the floor. Tomás shrugged his shoulders. Pete stared at me. "Why don't we go to the police?" I asked.

"They'd laugh at us," Tomás said. "We don't have one single concrete fact to tell them. What we had better do is more detecting. Pete and I will scout around that High Street house tomorrow after school."

"You're not being a bit bright," I objected. "You didn't see the car, and you're apt to have Jim Block trailing you. Jean and I will do the gumshoe bit. We can check the place without Jim knowing about it because we're out of school half an hour earlier than you."

Jean looked as if I'd volunteered her for a moon flight. Tomás' face settled into big brother lines, but Pete came to my defense. "No one will pay any attention to two girls on their way home from school. Nancy's smart enough not to get into trouble. Then we'll all meet at your grandparents' house and plan the next step."

Jean stood up. "My next step right now is home, and I'm afraid to go out the door. What if Jim is still sitting there?"

Tomás reached for his jacket. "I'll walk you home."

Pete stretched and pulled on his sweater. "Time for me to leave. I'll provide double protection."

Jean waved at me and giggled as she walked out between two escorts. I had a funny, shaky feeling as they left. Was Jean really scared or had she maneuvered Tomás and Pete into walking her home? I hoped Jean wasn't going to turn into one of those silly, giggling girls who widened their eyes at every boy they saw. Then I laughed at myself. What would Jean say when the news got around that Pete and I were going together, I wondered.

𝟛𝟶𝟬𝟛𝟶 **18** 𝟛𝟶𝟬𝟛𝟶

Somehow the idea of going to High Street was not as appealing the next day. I had an all gone feeling in the pit of my stomach. My hands were clammy, and I was certain I had the beginning of a sore throat. At noon I told Jean I thought we should go directly to my grandmother's.

"Tomás and Pete will call us a pair of silly girls," she said. "There's really no reason to be afraid. Nothing can happen to us in broad daylight on a busy street."

High Street wasn't at all busy when we turned the corner of the block where the large old house was. The afternoon was dark and dreary, the kind of day when one can almost smell the coming rain. I hoped Grandmother had found a roofer in need of work. A cold wind whipped leaves down the street. A couple of cars were parked in front of the house, but no blue-and-white station wagon.

We reached the walk leading to the sagging porch which was festooned with rotting gingerbread. No one was in sight. I took a deep breath, then hurried up the steps and looked at the mailboxes. Apartment number one said Wright. Number two said C. Brighton. Number three said Krysik. Number four was marked Seymour.

I scuttled back to the sidewalk. "Someone named Seymour lives in apartment four, but that still doesn't prove anything," I said.

Jean was bouncing a tennis ball on the sidewalk. "Come on," she ordered and walked a few steps to the driveway. "Catch!" she shouted and threw the ball over my shoulder up the driveway. Then she raced by me after the ball.

I stood there staring until she came back with an angry look on her face. "Butterfingers," she said loudly. "You might have made me lose my good tennis ball." She strode down the block with big steps and I hurried after her. We turned the corner.

"What are you so mad about?" I asked. "You can't expect me to catch a ball one-handed."

Jean had a bright smile on her face. "I'm not angry. That was just part of my detective act."

"You might have warned me," I began, then

stopped, realizing what her smug smile meant. "Was the station wagon back there?"

"It sure was. The same blue-and-white one you saw at the flea market."

"Did you see anything in it?"

Jean shook her head. "Just a couple of empty boxes in the back."

"You didn't see any belts or afghans?" I persisted.

"No. Just empty boxes."

I sighed. If there had been some evidence in the station wagon we could have called the police. Now we would have to do some more detecting, but I just didn't know what it would be. I hoped Tomás and Pete would have some ideas.

When we reached Grandmother's house, we saw a truck with a sign "Martin Roofing Service" parked in front. Jean and I grinned at each other and hurried inside. At least we wouldn't have to worry about the rain.

We found Grandmother sitting in the kitchen hard at work on an afghan. She stopped to pour us steaming cups of hot chocolate flavored with cinnamon. "How was school?" she asked.

"Oh, as usual." I picked up the afghan. "Pretty."

She went back to her rocker. "I'm hoping to finish three before Sunday. Then I can take them to the flea market when we go with the Olssens." Her fingers flew as she resumed work with the bright red and white yarns.

I blew on the steaming chocolate. "That'll be a lot of crocheting. Where's Grandfather?"

"Where would you expect? He's out back watching the roofers."

I nodded and reached for a cookie. Just then the back door opened and Tomás and Pete stalked in looking like a pair of angry dogs. Tomás' left eye was a deep purple.

Grandmother flew across the room to him. *"Madre de Dios, pobrecito.* Come, sit down. I'll get some ice for that eye."

"It's all right," Tomás said. "What I need is something for my stomach. It's empty."

Pete leaned against the door grinning at Tomás, who sat down at the kitchen table. "What on earth happened?" Jean asked.

Tomás looked at me with a face filled with anger. I backed away from the table. "What's the matter?"

"You! That's what! You and your big romance with Pete here," Tomás raged. "Do you think I want Jim Block flapping his lip about my sister all over the school?"

Grandmother's eyes were round with astonishment. I started to laugh and so did Pete.

"Jim Block gave you that black eye for a souvenir,

I suppose," I said when I could talk.

Tomás nodded.

"Men!" I exploded. "Dumb, stupid men. Why, you knew it was all an act. We talked it over before we left the house. I'll bet you hit him first."

Tomás had the grace to look sheepish. "Yeah, I got in a good lick, but I also caught a three-day suspension."

"Wow! You're going to have a tough time explaining that to the parents."

Grandmother gave him a comforting hug and handed him a plate filled with *polvorones*. She didn't ask any questions, which surprised me. After a moment's thought, I realized that Grandmother usually waited patiently until we explained things.

My eye caught Pete's and we were off on another gale of laughter. Then I settled down and smiled at Tomás. "You should have caught Jean's act this afternoon. You'd have thought she was Chris Evert."

"Is it the right place?" Tomás asked, leaning forward intently.

Jean and I nodded.

"Now what?" Pete's face was alive with excitement.

I shrugged. We looked from one to the other, knowing that we couldn't talk about the problem any more in front of Grandmother.

"I've been doing some more sorting in the attic,"

she said brightly. "I found another box filled with your father's belongings, Tomás. It's a big box just to the right of the attic door. Maybe you would like to go up and bring it downstairs."

"What's in it?" Tomás asked.

"Mostly old toys. Some of them windup."

The word "windup" caught my attention. "Let's all go," I said and picked up the antique price guide on my way through the dining room.

When we reached the attic, we realized we wouldn't

be able to talk there. The noise from the roof was deafening. "Let's take the box down to the kitchen," Tomás suggested. He picked it up and started for the stairs.

"We need to have a private planning session, Tomás," I said.

"Okay, but we can't have it here. All we would do is plan ourselves into some headaches."

When we reached the kitchen, Grandmother shook her head. "I'm starting dinner, and I don't want all of you underfoot. Try the living room."

I picked up some newspapers and a dust cloth in case the toys were dirty and we went into the living room.

Tomás put the box down and turned to me. "What did you find out?"

"The station wagon is parked behind the house. Jean saw it. So what are we going to do now?"

"Is their name on the mailbox?" Pete asked.

Jean smiled proudly. "Nancy sneaked up on the porch and looked. Seymour was the name on apartment four."

"That's probably upstairs and complicates matters," Tomás said. "The problem is how to get into the apartment."

Pete's mouth dropped open. "You're not serious about breaking and entering! That could get us into trouble."

"Not if we find the stolen goods there. We could hang around and see when those Seymours leave. Maybe they don't even lock their door," Tomás argued.

While they talked, I had started unpacking the box. I pulled out a Mickey Mouse windup tin racing car and a wooden jigsaw puzzle. There were three other racing cars and a mechanical bear holding an ear of corn. I set the bear on the floor and turned the key. He

166

danced and the ear of corn revolved in his hands.

Jean laughed and picked up the dancing bear. "He's cute."

"Too bad we didn't know about these things years ago," Tomás said. "We're a bit past the pull toy and racing-car stage."

I was leafing through the price guide. "Here. Look at this. Disney collectibles. Windup tin racing car. Forty-two dollars. Dad has a fortune here!"

"He'll say they belong to Grandmother, and she'll say they are his," Tomás said. He pulled a funny-looking machine out of the box.

"What's that?" I asked.

"A steam engine, dummy."

"Don't call me a dummy. How would I know? I never saw a toy steam engine before."

I turned the pages to toys and found brass steam engines listed at thirty-five to fifty dollars. "Is that brass?"

"It looks like it," Tomás answered. "I wonder what Dad will want to do with these old toys?"

"The point is what are we going to do about the Seymours?" Jean said. "We have to come up with a better idea than breaking and entering."

"Why not just forget about it?" Pete suggested. "Your grandparents are having the roof fixed, so the problem is solved."

Tomás' face darkened. "You forget my Apache blood. The problem isn't solved when that ratty-faced guy is getting away with stealing from old people. Our honor has been smirched." Tomás looked just like Grandfather as he glared at Pete.

"We could go back to the flea market," I said.

Jean looked ready to cry. "Nancy, I don't think I could face that highway. I'm having trouble even getting into a car."

I knew exactly how she felt. My insides started earthquaking at the thought, but I couldn't come up with a better idea. "With the four of us, those Seymours couldn't get away like they did before. But how would we get there? There wouldn't be room in the Olssens' car."

"We could take the bus," Tomás said.

Jean looked at him as if he had just come up with a theory to revolutionize space flight. "What a great idea! I think I could face that highway on a big bus."

Tomás shrugged and, with a morose look, pulled his headband from his pocket. "I keep thinking about Jim," he said, looking first at me, then at Pete. "What if we prove the Seymours are thieves, and they implicate Jim? I think I should talk to him, warn him. I can't stand the idea of getting a friend in trouble. That's not being loyal."

"Hold on, Tomás. You're getting your priorities

wrong," Pete warned. "If you talk to Jim and he *is* mixed up with those thieves, we'll never find your grandparents' property."

"Remember the accident and the way he treated Nancy. I can't see why you should feel any loyalty toward him," Jean said.

"But if he's in trouble, he needs friends, and I'm his friend," Tomás insisted stubbornly.

Pete picked up the dancing bear and wound it. "We don't know that Jim is in trouble, but we don't stand a chance of solving this case if you tell him what we're planning."

"Okay, I'll keep quiet, but I won't feel right about it." Tomás rolled up the headband and shoved it into his pocket.

"You haven't been wearing your headband lately, Tomás." Pete's voice sounded curious.

"I don't need it."

"What do you mean by that?" I asked.

"The more I read about the Apaches and the California Indians at the time the Missions were established, and the Spanish who colonized Mexico and California, the prouder I am of all my ancestors," Tomás explained. "Also I've realized that I'm me, and what *I* do is what counts. This business with Jim has made me do a lot of thinking."

"Wow! What a speech!" Jean applauded. "That

would be a great closing for a play."

Tomás shrugged. "Forget it. Next week I may start carrying the shillelagh that Nancy once suggested."

I smiled at my brother. And, for the first time since the accident, I really hoped that Jim Block wasn't involved in the robbery of the Co-op.

🎔🎔 19 🎔🎔

We left the Santo Rosario bus depot at eight o'clock the following Sunday morning. Tomás, Pete, Jean, and I found seats together in the rear. Jean had a floppy beach hat in her hand. "I'm not going to get sunburned this time," she explained.

"Who could get sunburned in November?" I asked.

"I could," Jean said. "I did the last time we went to the flea market."

"Do we split up when we get there?" Pete directed his question at me.

"Let's stay together," I said. "If we find those crooks, it will take all four of us to keep them from getting away."

Jean squirmed uneasily on the stiff seat. "What if they aren't there? Maybe we're taking this trip for nothing."

"Then we'll have a nice day at the flea market," I answered. "We'll look first at the place where they were before. Mrs. Olssen told me that people who are regular sellers like to get the same spot each time or one as near it as possible. That way their steady customers can find them."

"Tomás, what did your father say about the racing cars and windup bear?" Pete asked.

"He laughed. Then he put the box in the back of his closet. Mom let out a few moans about another pack rat," Tomás said.

"It's a good thing Grandmother and I are pack rats," I said, complacently.

The bus rolled easily along the freeway toward Los Olivos. As we neared the summit, I felt fear clutching at my stomach. The bad curves were just ahead of us. Jean's face was white, and her eyes were closed. I looked at Tomás. He grinned at me and reached for Jean's hand. "Did I ever tell you about the day Pete and I went stalking through these mountains and saw a great grizzly bear?" he asked in a low, growly voice.

"No, you didn't."

"The bear was bigger than a rhinoceros. He reared up on his hind legs and looked at us. He opened his mouth and roared like a lion. Then he said, 'I'm going to eat you two boys up.' "

Jean started to laugh. "Tomás, bears don't talk."

"This one did. He said we were trespassing on his mountain, didn't he, Pete?"

"He sure did. Then he stretched out a great purple paw at us." Pete spoke the words in a quavery voice.

"Then what happened?" Jean asked.

"He ate us up," Tomás said.

I giggled; then I roared with laughter. "As a story-teller, you're a flop, Tomás." My eyes met his, and I smiled, proud of my brother. We were past the second curve, and Jean relaxed.

We reached the flea market entrance at ten-thirty, after a ride on the city bus. "The station-wagon people were at the end of my second row. That was the fourth row because you had the first two, Tomás," I said.

"Okay, we'll start there, but we'll approach the place cautiously."

We made our way through the crowd to the end of the row. There was no sign of a blue-and-white station wagon. My shoulders sagged. "This is where they were. I'm certain of it." I turned to a man sitting behind a green card table. "There are usually some people here with a blue-and-white station wagon. They had some lovely crocheted afghans. Do you know where they might be?"

"Oh, they were late getting here this morning so

they are over at the other end. Pretty afghans, aren't they? He must have a lot of old ladies working for him."

I thanked the man and we started across the flea market. "We might be on the wrong track. He could be getting those afghans and sweaters on consignment," Jean suggested. "I know a girl in high school who makes macramé plant hangers for gift shops on consignment."

"Remember the belts?" Tomás kicked a paper napkin out of his way, then bent over, picked it up, and put it in a trash can.

We reached the last row of flea market dealers and looked cautiously down the aisle. I could see no sign of a blue-and-white station wagon. We went along the row, inspecting each display carefully, but saw no belts or crocheted items.

"Let's try the row before this one. We know they are here," I said.

We rounded the corner. I saw the station wagon three stalls down. Buck Seymour stood behind a table covered with handicrafted items. I didn't see the girl.

"Come on," I said. I hurried to the table and started looking through the afghans. There it was, orange and gray, edged with Grandmother's special stitch, and in the corner I found the tiny LP that she used to sign her work.

"It's only twenty-five dollars," Buck Seymour drawled. "That's a mighty good price for a handmade afghan."

On the next pile I spotted a heavy yellow and white sweater with intricate Aztec designs. I'd watched *mi abuelita* make that sweater! On the right front edge, I found the LP. Tomás was beside me, and I held it out to him.

"That one's only ten dollars," Buck said. "You won't find a better deal anywhere." He looked at me intently, his forehead wrinkled. "Don't I know you?"

I exploded. "No, you don't, but I know you. You're a thief! You steal from old people living on pensions."

"Now wait a minute. Don't you go around calling people names like that. I could sue you," he whined. "I have people working for me who supply this merchandise."

"My grandmother doesn't work for you, and she made this." I held up the sweater. "You stole this from the Senior Citizens' Co-op in Santo Rosario."

Buck snorted. "I've never been in Santo Rosario in my life."

Tomás and Pete dashed around the table to the open back of the station wagon. "Hey, what are you doing?" Buck shouted and shoved Tomás. "Get out of there."

Tomás ducked and held up a hand-tooled leather wallet. "Isn't this one of Grandfather's?" he asked.

"Look for the little *p* inside the cover," I said.

Buck snatched it from Tomás' hand. "You punks get away from here!" he roared.

People crowded around us. "What's going on?" a man yelled. Buck shoved Tomás, and Tomás shoved him back. The girl with the braids pushed her way through the crowd and grabbed Tomás' arm. Then she saw me and her eyes widened. So did mine. She was wearing the hammered silver bracelet—the bracelet Mr. Jackson had made.

She backed away toward the car, and I ran around the table. "That's Mr. Jackson's bracelet!" I shouted. "Give it back."

She opened the front door of the car and I reached for her arm. As she twisted away, I clonked her on the shoulder with my cast. She slid to the ground, and Jean sat on her legs. I started to pull at the bracelet, but Jean stopped me. "Leave the evidence where it is."

The girl tried to get up and bumped her head against the fender. I grabbed one of the long braids and pulled it hard. "Stay right here!" I ordered.

"Ouch! Stop it. Let me go," she pleaded.

"What are you doing?" a loud voice demanded. I looked up. A security guard stood beside me, glaring at me. "We can't have fights here."

"They started it," the girl said.

"They are thieves!" I shouted. "This stuff is all stolen."

"You can't prove anything. Let go of me!" Buck Seymour yelled, struggling to get away from Tomás and Pete, who held him by the arms. "These kids are just trying to make trouble," he added in a lower voice.

The security guard looked from Buck Seymour to me doubtfully.

"Those afghans and sweaters were stolen from the Senior Citizens' Co-op in Santo Rosario," I said excitedly. "We can prove it. *Mi abuelita* made them, and she's here at the flea market. With the Olssens."

"I know the Olssens," the guard said. "They are a nice couple. Who's *Abuelita?*"

"*Mi abuelita es Abuelita.* Oh, I mean my grandmother. My grandfather is here, too."

He turned to Buck Seymour. "Let me see your driver's license."

"You've got no authority over me," Buck protested. His face had turned a dull gray.

"We'll see about that!" The guard beckoned to another security man standing at the edge of the now quiet crowd. "Joe, call the police. Then find the Olssens and bring the people with them back here."

In moments my grandparents were beside us and so

were the police. Grandmother identified her afghan and sweater. "Rose Lawrence made that quilt," she said, pointing to a quilt covered with blocks of appliquéd leaves.

"That girl is wearing Mr. Jackson's bracelet," I said, then looked with dismay at her bare arm. "She had it on when she was getting into the car," I insisted.

Then I saw a gleam behind the rear tire. I bent over and picked up the bracelet. "Mr. Jackson made it," I said, handing it to the officer.

"Nancy, what have you done to your cast?" Grandmother was staring at me with horror.

I looked at my cast. It was broken at the elbow. "I clonked her with it."

"We must get you to a doctor right away and have it fixed," she said.

"It doesn't hurt and it's coming off soon, anyway. Some adhesive tape will mend it." I saw the officer putting handcuffs on Buck Seymour. Then he ordered Buck and the girl into the back of a patrol car.

"We'll contact the Santo Rosario police," the officer said to my grandparents. "Right now everything on the table and in the back of the wagon is evidence, but you'll get your property back soon."

Grandfather nodded. "Mrs. Lancet, the manager of the Co-op, keeps records on all consignments. She can identify these things."

"We'll be in touch with her," the officer promised. "You'll have to come to the station and sign a statement before you leave town." The security guard drove the station wagon away, and we followed my grandparents back to the Olssens' stall.

"How are you doing?" I asked Grandmother.

"I've sold two of Great-aunt Maria's vases for thirty dollars each. Your grandfather is doing fine with his belts, but I haven't sold any afghans. People say the price is too high."

"What are you asking?"

"Fifty dollars."

I grinned and looked at Jean. "Make you a good deal, lady," she singsonged in an imitation of Buck Seymour's drawl. "Only twenty-five dollars."

"What are you talking about?" Grandmother asked.

"You were in competition with yourself," I explained. "That thief was selling your afghans for half your price."

Grandmother was aghast. "Twenty-five dollars! That barely pays for the yarn."

Customers were crowded in front of the Olssens' table, and I realized we would be in the way. "Let's get some lunch," I said to Tomás. "Then catch the bus back. We're all finished here."

"Okay, but I want to talk to some book dealers before we leave. Maybe we can interest one of them in the rest of the Big Little Books."

We agreed and Tomás and Pete started off at a brisk pace. Jean and I followed, but my steps lagged. "We still don't know if Jim was involved in the robbery," I said.

"He had to be," Jean answered adamantly. "How else can you explain his knowing those crooks?"

"I don't know." We caught up with Tomás and Pete at a bookseller's stall, and I didn't dare say anything more. I knew that my brother would be terribly upset if Jim turned out to be a thief.

❧❧❧ 20 ❧❧❧

O n the way to Grandmother's house after school
the next afternoon, Jean gave me a questioning
look. "You've changed a lot," she said, much to my
surprise.

"Me?" I asked, incredulous. "I'm just the same bum-
bling, tongue-tied me."

"No, you're not. You shouted at that guard, and you
clonked that girl. Today you even answered a question
in government class without your usual ah-eh-oh beginning."

"I'd better watch that. I'll get a reputation for being
a chatterbox."

"Not you," Jean said with her soft laugh. "But you
seem somewhat loosened up. Easier with people."

I walked along in silence, thinking about her words.
Had I really changed? Maybe I had. For one thing, I

was considering joining the police force when I grew up, instead of being an engineer.

I glanced up at the new roof as we reached the house and smiled at Jean. "I'm sure glad we met the Olssens."

She nodded and we hurried inside. My grandparents were sitting at the kitchen table drinking coffee. Grandmother poured milk for us, then handed me a sealed envelope and a small package wrapped in white tissue paper.

"What's this?" I asked.

"The money we owe you is in the envelope. All of it," Grandfather said.

"You didn't make *that* much money at the flea market!"

Grandfather shook his head and looked at my grandmother.

"We sold the oak dining-room set!" she explained. "That nice young man who came to the garage sale came back last night. He offered three hundred dollars and I took it. I know Mrs. Olssen said I could probably get more, but I liked that young man. He's getting married," she finished with a smile.

I smiled back at her. I realized Grandmother was picturing the happy couple having dinner at Great-aunt Maria's table.

Jean nudged me. "Aren't you going to open the package?"

I tore off the wrapping and gulped when I saw the dull gleam of a hammered silver bracelet. "Th-thank you," I stammered, my tongue going into knots. "But, but—"

"The members of the Co-op had a meeting with the police this morning. They recovered about half our property. The Seymours had disposed of the rest of it. Their apartment was full of stolen goods. Some from the Co-op, some from houses that they'd broken into. Television sets, stereos, jewelry, tape decks. They had a big operation going," Grandfather said.

I looked at the bracelet shining on my arm. "You haven't explained about this."

"The Co-op members decided you should have a reward. Bill Jackson had made another bracelet and we all chipped in and bought it for you, Nancy." She turned to Jean. "You're to pick out something at the Co-op."

Jean smiled happily. "I already know what I want. One of your sweaters, a blue one. Whenever Nan calls you *Abuelita*, I think of you as *Abuelita Crochet* because that's what you are always doing. I've wanted one of your sweaters for ages."

The back door opened and I stared in amazement as

Tomás, Pete, and Jim Block entered the kitchen.

"Close your mouth, Nan," Tomás ordered. "Teachers' meeting. They let us out early."

Still speechless, I looked at Jim. His face slowly reddened as Tomás introduced him to the grandparents. "I—I came to apologize," Jim said in a husky voice. "My father said I had to, but I would have anyway."

"Apologize. Why?" Grandfather's tone was stern.

"For everything. The trouble I've caused. The accident." He hesitated and choked.

Grandmother smiled kindly at him. "Sit down and explain."

Jim continued to stand, looking first at Grandmother, then at Grandfather. "Well, I knew the Seymours were crooks when I saw them at the flea market. Tomás had described the belts and your afghans, Mrs. Pérez, but I was afraid to turn them in. Instead, I told Buck that the cops were searching the flea market for stolen goods."

Grandmother took a quick sharp breath. Grandfather's face darkened. "Why did you do that?"

"I didn't want them to know Nancy was hunting for the stolen goods. They're mean characters and I was afraid they'd cause trouble for her—maybe even hurt her."

"But why did you warn them at all?" I asked.

"I know I was stupid, but I guess I thought if I did them a favor, they'd let me off the hook. You see, they had something on me. I'd had a previous accident. Just a small one. Dented a fender with my bumper after drinking a few beers. I knew my father would be furious because the insurance rate would go up, so I asked the other driver not to report the accident and I paid the damage."

He stopped and looked down at his shoes. Tomás gave him an encouraging pat on the shoulder. "Come on, Jim. Tell them the rest of it."

"Well, Buck Seymour had seen the accident. He told the other man to sue me and offered to be a witness. The man laughed at him and drove off. Then Buck said he'd tell my father unless I gave him a twenty."

Grandmother gasped. "Such awful people! Blackmailers as well as thieves."

Jim nodded and swallowed hard. "Then Buck phoned me, demanding more money. I had to pay for the wine and beer for those parties at Two Mile Beach. He was always asking for a five or ten." Jim turned to me. "That's why you saw me with him at the boardwalk."

I smiled at him, remembering his anger when Buck

asked me to go to the beach party. "But what were you doing at their house?"

"Buck had called me and demanded more money. I didn't dare go up to their apartment while you and Pete were around because I was afraid you'd think I was mixed-up with them."

"I did," Jean said frankly. "Besides, your wild driving caused our accident."

"I had a couple of beers after I left you that day at the flea market. I was so confused I thought I needed them," he admitted, his face troubled. "Believe me, I'm off beer."

Deep inside I felt a surge of admiration for Jim as he stood there looking at us. Tomás had been right. Jim did have good qualities. How hard it must have been for him to come here and apologize!

"After Tomás phoned me last night to tell me the Seymours had been caught red-handed, I decided to tell my father the whole story, even to borrowing his car after I'd lost my license. You know, he didn't shout at me at all? He just said I should have come to him in the beginning, and he seemed sad." Jim sounded puzzled.

"Sometimes parents surprise their children," Grandmother murmured gently.

Jim nodded. "Anyway, that's what happened and I *am* sorry."

"You didn't have to tell your father, Jim. Why did you do that?" I asked.

"I just couldn't stand things the way they were with my parents hardly talking to me, so I decided to tell them everything that had happened. I'm glad I did because Dad said I'd been acting even more aloof and strange after the accident and they were worried about me. I'm sorry about everything," he repeated.

I sprang up from my chair and took him by the arm. "Come and sit down and don't feel so bad. If you hadn't been mixed-up with those people we would never have found out they were the thieves."

"Right, Jim. You helped us find them," Tomás said. "And there's one other piece of unfinished business." He nodded to me and pulled out his billfold.

I opened my shoulder bag and took out the four rolled belts that I'd been carrying since that first day at the flea market. I handed them to Grandfather and Tomás gave him the money.

"Where—how did you get these?" Grandfather asked.

"The Seymours had sold some of your stolen belts to the Olssens. We couldn't tell you. We were afraid you'd suspect them and notify the police," I explained.

"Suspect that nice lady!" Grandmother sounded horrified.

"I'm starving, *Abuelita*," Tomás announced. "Is the cookie jar full?"

Grandmother nodded. She brought the clear glass cookie jar over to the table. It was filled to the top with *spritz baklese*.

ABOUT THE AUTHOR

VIRGINIA B. EVANSEN was born in Havre, Montana, attended school in Portland, Oregon, and Saginaw, Michigan, and was graduated from the University of Michigan.

Mrs. Evansen presently teaches Writing Autobiography for Cabrillo College Community Services. She is a member of the National League of American Pen Women and is state president (California North). In addition to four books, she has written over a hundred magazine articles, short stories, and features.

Besides Oregon and Michigan, the author has lived in Sunnyvale, California. While there, Mrs. Evansen was appointed to the Public Library Board of Trustees and served two years as Board Chairman. She was a charter member of the Sunnyvale Friends of the Library.

The author is married to Kenneth M. Evansen, an engineer. They reside in Santa Cruz, California, and have three daughters, Virginia Ann, Patricia, and Nancy.

ABOUT THE ARTIST

RAY ABEL lives in Scarsdale, New York. In addition to his many jackets and book illustrations, his work has been exhibited in group art shows, and he has made five sketching trips to Europe and Africa.